They're back,
they're online,
and
they mean
business.

darkcorp.com

flambeau@darkcorp.com

darkcorp.com
darkcorp.com

DON HAWKINS

kregel
PUBLICATIONS

Grand Rapids, MI 49501

flambeau@darkcorp.com

Published by Kregel Publications, a division of Kregel, Inc., P.O. Box 2607, Grand Rapids, MI 49501. Kregel Publications provides trusted, biblical publications for Christian growth and service. Your comments and suggestions are valued.

Cover and book design: Nicholas G. Richardson

ISBN 0-8254-2868-9

Printed in the United States of America

1 2 3 / 04 03 02 01 00 99

PREFACE

"Without an original there can be no imitation" is a phrase that perfectly describes my debt to C. S. Lewis. I am one of a vast number of Lewis fans who not only enjoys his inimitable and truly original writing style but also has grown spiritually from his insights.

His works continue to be discovered by succeeding generations since his death in 1963 (in one of those odd historical coincidences, on the same day that John F. Kennedy was killed). In Lewis's classic *The Screwtape Letters,* a demon uncle writes a series of directives to his pernicious demon nephew, instructing him in the finer points of "the wiles of the devil." Lewis referred to his style as "moral inversion," the deliberate reversal of the holy and unholy wherein lies are spoken as if they were true and truth is treated as a lie.

Whereas *The Screwtape Letters* focused primarily on an individual and his inner spiritual life, my goal is to examine the local church, the foundation of God's work on earth today. Jesus pointed out that one of the Enemy's purposes is to sow weeds among the wheat (Matt. 13:24–30). My objective is to demonstrate how Satan might seek to disrupt the body of believers by counterfeiting the spiritual gifts given by the Lord to individual members of his body, gifts such as serving, teaching, encouraging, giving, leading, and showing mercy (Rom. 12:6–8).

Lewis described hell as "something like the bureaucracy of a police state or the offices of a thoroughly nasty business concern."[1] I've chosen to take the latter comparison to its highest (or perhaps lowest!) development at the end of the twentieth century—the modern multinational business corporation. Such an operation is often considered to be "hell" by those who work under the constant threat of demotion and downsizing, combined with a "succeed at any cost" mentality and the all-too-human passion to dominate and control others. What if it really was hell?

While I'm indebted to Lewis for the model, my own vision of this devilish enterprise makes no pretense of "family." With Satan himself as the Chief Executive Officer, this corporation is run by status-conscious (but conscience- deficient) demons with cutthroat efficiency. Since they are technologically savvy, e-mail is their preferred mode of communication. Scraptus, the Vice President for North American Operations, instructs Flambeau, who has just been appointed to the position of regional manager in the Counter Operations Division. Flambeau has been using some of Satan's tried-and-true methods from the past; but corporate changes have occurred in the evil empire, and a new emphasis on diabolical gifts has been instituted. This correspondence could best be described as "An Operations Manual for Diabolic Activity in the Local Church."

My collection of counterfeit gifts is somewhat arbitrary but reflects my experience as a pastor and counselor. Unfortunately, it's not uncommon to meet individuals in the church who are extremely skilled in criticism, manipulation, gossip, discouragement, intimidation, deceit, or the other "gifts" described in this book. While the situations and actions described are accurate to life, all the characters and events are fictional, and any resemblance to persons living or dead is coincidental. I also recognize, as Lewis did, that coming up with these examples doesn't take a lot of study. As he put it, "My heart—I need no other's—showeth me the wickedness of the ungodly."[2]

I've chosen to write this book as fiction rather than as a biblical, theological exposition for a simple reason: As Lewis demonstrated, we sometimes gain greater benefit by looking at things from an angle with which we are not familiar. I hope that viewing these issues from the enemy's perspective will help us become more keenly aware of the reality of the spiritual warfare in which we live and operate as Christians.

We may also have to face the unpleasant reality that we have been guilty from time to time of adopting the same strategies applied by the demonic heroes of this work. The remedy for the pain occasioned by such a discovery is not difficult to find. God's Word promises, "If we confess our sins, He is faithful and just to forgive us our sins and to cleanse us from all unrighteousness" (1 John 1:9).

Furthermore, I want to help us identify with and relate to those who, at work, in the community, and in the church, may have become proficient in using these diabolical skills. Our first instinct may be to avoid them, but our biblical responsibility is to speak the truth in love to them. Our ultimate goal as believers is to move beyond the works of the flesh and consistently display the fruit of the Spirit and the true gifts of God's grace to the church.

darkcorp.com

flambeau@darkcorp.com

darkcorp.com

darkcorp.com

>>CONFIDENTIAL MEMO ONE<<

To: flambeau@darkcorp.com
From: scraptus@darkcorp.com
Subject: Your New Initiative (Foundational Strategy)

Better you hear the bad news from me than from someone else like Hotspur: You are in serious trouble. Your client has not only embraced our Competitor's enterprise but also has become involved in one of their local business units. What a disaster!

I can't believe that after so many years of success you've let him get away. You managed to divert his attention from the Competition's Business Plan (what they quaintly call the "Bible") he received in the Marines. You even kept him from that military buddy who joined the Competitor's acquisition team. And now, just when things were getting easy, you've let him fall under the influence of a woman from the Competition! Clearly you failed to recognize the danger of his vulnerability after the death of his first wife. With little or no opposition, you permitted him to become entangled in the spiderlike web of a widow who has loved and served the Competition for decades. What were you thinking? Did you fall asleep at your keyboard, Flambeau? Our CEO Below doesn't tolerate such lapses in judgment. You're in danger of demotion to some Satan-forsaken outpost with the career potential of a cold virus!

However, if you'll pay attention, I can suggest some ways to turn this hostile takeover into an acquisition—and in the process leave our Competitor fighting more brush fires than even he can deal with. After all, our Chairman has always been gifted at takeovers, raids, and leverage actions of all kinds. Let me explain what I have in mind.

Your client, Gene, is now officially classified as one of the Competition's employees, which makes it much more difficult for you to influence his thinking and behavior. However, he and others like him, including his associates who attend the Local Competition Unit in Glencrest (LCU to us and "Glencrest Bible Church" to them) still have the capability of following the motivations and behaviors of our CEO Below. What we have to counter is the internal influence of the Competition's Spirit, the so-called encourager of those who follow our Competitor closely, and, perhaps most dangerous of all, the influence of that powerful Business Manual they call a lamp to their feet and a light to their path—whatever that means. The "light" metaphor is obviously repugnant. Our CEO's forces have been trying to stamp out that book for centuries. We've been gaining in recent years; the market share of this work has dropped drastically during the last few decades, so we must be succeeding.

However, the major issue is not how many of these books are purchased but how many get used. Our Debased Head Honcho would prefer that many of them be acquired then set on a shelf to gather dust. That's better than having only a few purchased but each of them carefully studied and then implemented.

A major part of your objective, Flambeau, will be to disrupt the influence of this insidious document, which contains their business plan and threatens to break our grip on those who have been acquired by our Competitor.

More to the point is the strategic benefit I want you to see in counterfeiting the tactics of the Competition in building up his Local Competition Unit, weak and disunified though it may be. That's why I'm broadening your assignment from simply working with Gene to moving freely among all the members of the LCU at Glencrest. They're all our takeover targets now. You are hereby empowered to employ the gifts of our Chairman in such a way as can best hinder the gifts of our Competitor to his LCU. I don't have to tell you that the more effectively you can motivate the members of your particular sphere of influence to adopt and practice the gifts of our Infernal CEO, the greater your potential for personal reward and promotion.

I'm sure you are aware—and if you aren't, Flambeau, you should be—of the prominent role played by my mentor, Calamdus. As you know, he has the ear of our Maleficent Founder; in fact, he was charged by his Exalted Darkness with the responsibility of refining these diabolical gifts for the postmodern world. We realized that the most effective way to attack the Competition was to counterfeit his strategies and activities. That's why our Chairman assigned Calamdus the task of developing particular abilities, based on human tendencies, that could counter the supernatural forces of the Spirit of our Competition. The spreadsheets released by the Head Office Below indicate that Calamdus has done a masterful job, so this memo and others following it will be based to a great degree on strategic concepts I learned from him at a management seminar some time ago.

To assist you in your debased responsibility, I'm thinking of collecting this and several future memos into a handbook that you and others can use to implement our corporate plan. In future communiqués, I will be referencing the Competition's Business Plan—both their Current Business Plan or CBP (their "New Testament"), and their Previous Business Plan or PBP (archaically called the "Old Testament"). I plan to include certain footnotes for your benefit and to meet the standards of infernal scholarship established by His Debased Eminence. He used both accurate and less than accurate quotations from the Competition's Business Plan in his most celebrated attempts to subvert both the first miserable pair of humans and the Competition's CEO designate. Since this approach may be misconstrued by some in the lower ranks (who are no doubt destined to remain there, given their outdated practices), let's keep this exchange confidential.

I'm doing this in spite of my reluctance to make such extensive use of their Business Plan. Like most of the other members of our acquisition staff, you're probably quite unfamiliar with it and rightly so. Its language and concepts are obsolete—hardly worth using up any memory in that smart demonic brain of yours. However, I think you would be wise to spend time brushing up on this antiquated document. Let me explain.

Before the 1960s, most humans gave at least a measure of respect to the Competition's Business Plan. However, our infernal research department put together a counter-effort that emphasized various cultural trends—Eastern religions, existential literary works, and pop culture icons. The result: a sexual and social revolution that led most humans to the conclusion that our Competition's Business Plan was just another in a long series of mankind's documents with little or no value for contemporary human life.

I still hesitate to point you to their Business Plan, which (as you may recall from your historical studies) was required for study and use by an earlier generation of our diabolical team. However, given the fact that your mission is one of infiltration and subversion, I think it is essential that you know the enemy. This means that you must understand the outmoded vocabulary they frequently employ—even if they don't always understand the significance of it themselves. After all, if you are to succeed, you must understand everything about the Competition so you can pinpoint and take advantage of each weakness.

I should not have to remind you that dire consequences await if you fail to carry out this mission. And don't think for a minute that you have any choice in the matter. If you reject this assignment you will self-destruct in five seconds or less! So devote your energies to mastering the skills I will explain in my following memos. Develop a master plan for using these assets to their most effective ends: to disrupt the growth and strategies of Gene and the rest of the Competition's people as well as their efforts to acquire those who have remained loyal under our corporate banner. We simply cannot allow their attack on our client market to go unchallenged.

If you are to fulfill your mission successfully, you must have some insight into the thinking the Competition has foisted on his people about the skills our Competitor refers to as "spiritual gifts." A powerful directive written by their corporate leader Paul, one of their most ruthless raiders, to the Competition's employees in Ephesus indicated that spiritual gifts were a "divine enablement," an ability bestowed by the Competitor himself for serving both the Competition and humanity. Our Pernicious Boss has instructed us to defuse the impact of these gifts by suggesting that activities such as baking pies, playing the piano, traveling to a foreign country, or working with children are "gifts." Still, it seems that more of the Competition's followers are coming to understand—and worse, to use—these abilities endowed by our Adversary. That's why it's imperative that we counter the works of their so-called Spirit with some of our finest fleshly marketed products.

As you know, our Debased Founder has instituted numerous modifications in our organizational structure in recent years. As the Chairman and CEO for our far-flung and multifaceted international organization, he has improved the lines of communication and recently promoted my mentor, Calamdus, to the position of Vice President of International Operations, in charge of all daily efforts to disrupt the Competition's strategies. He took this action primarily because of Calamdus's success in developing these diabolical gifts and training others to distribute them. Calamdus has appointed me to lead our North American efforts. The methods I'll suggest to you aren't new; in fact, we've been using them in one form or another for centuries. But, to be very candid, a new generation of those feeble, inept creatures called humans has arisen. Because of cultural changes and what they perceive as spiritual bankruptcy, they have become more interested in whatever the Competition might have to offer that will give meaning to their lives.

You must therefore appeal to their baser instincts and to memories of their misspent youth. Clearly the same things that attracted them, the things our Competition refers to as temptations, have of necessity been upgraded in recent days. Many more resources, including the Internet, the motion picture industry, and cable television, are available to our Founder and his loyal team, and we have high-placed representatives looking out for our interests in each of these areas. We also have operatives strategically placed within key human corporations of North America, as we do in other parts of the world. We're encouraging everything from the drug trade to white-collar crime. All of these things are extremely useful to our CEO Below and his team of takeover raiders.

However, for those like Gene who have committed themselves to the Competition's agenda, our best approach is to utilize some of the basic drives that come so naturally to these human subjects—like criticism, gossip, and discouragement. The more you are able to stir such things into the mix as they gather together to pursue the Competition's Business Plan, the more effectively our own causes will be fulfilled. This should be a career-making opportunity, Flambeau. Once you have successfully implemented these strategies in your target LCU, you will be able to train and recruit others and supervise their activities.

I expect nothing less than brilliant success. Your corporate future is on the line. Hotspur has mentioned on several occasions how much he enjoys the view from your office. He thinks it suits him nicely. To be candid, I don't appreciate his methods; they're much more like the old school—not as modern or as subtle as mine—yet effective in their own quaint way. His tactics have been influenced by that old dinosaur Slerchus, who, as you know, was recently retired. That doesn't mean you shouldn't consider Hotspur a threat, even though he's not ready to move up to your level—unless, of course, a vacancy should arise.

Yours is an important mission. Don't allow yourself to shrink from this awesome opportunity. You'll certainly miss that lovely new office and those other perks of power if you do!

>>CONFIDENTIAL MEMO TWO<<

To: flambeau@darkcorp.com
From: scraptus@darkcorp.com
Subject: Using the Gift of Criticism

I'm pleased to hear of your willingness to undertake the strategic mission I've assigned you on behalf of our CEO Below. Now that you've had a chance to survey the market by circulating among the people of the LCU of Glencrest, you're undoubtedly aware that this is not a lost cause. Even though your client, Gene, has become an acquisition of this group and is beginning to show signs of growth in their so-called grace and knowledge, he is not yet beyond our influence.

I'm glad you agree with my suggestion that the key to disrupting Gene's growing competence (not to mention the function of this so-called Body) is to gain leverage by spreading our Pernicious Boss's arsenal of gifts.

You probably recall that one of the Competition's strongest assets is what he calls encouragement. This "gift of encouragement" purports to remove fear and replace it with courage—that's why our Competitor's followers call it en-courage-ment (disgusting concept, isn't it—en-fear-ment is what we're after!). They have the mistaken notion that they can infuse courage into the hearts of their followers through this weak and useless process.

We have developed many strategies to block these efforts, but none has been more effective than the gift of criticism. It is one of our most useful weapons. If I were to suggest a definition, Flambeau, I would probably call it the "extraordinary skill of identifying faults, dispensing shame, and belittling someone else while explaining one's own superior approach."

As you've noticed, Flambeau, there are three elements in my definition. Some potential clients will demonstrate a greater propensity for identifying faults; others will show more facility for dispensing shame and humiliation; and still others will be more effective at belittling others while informing them of a better way.

Let me give you an example or two to help you see how this works. Leonard is a member of the corporate board at LCU of Glencrest. You've probably noticed how sharply he dresses and the influential, articulate way he expresses himself to other members of the Competition's camp. Leonard also serves as the senior vice president of a large and growing human company, where he has been especially proficient at using his gift of criticism. Just the other day he came close to presenting us with a major coup. He had one of his division managers, Bill, so depressed that he was ready to commit suicide. As you know, Flambeau, the Top Guy Down Below awards special honors to anyone who motivates a client to take his own life.

It turns out that the man didn't go quite that far, but let me tell you what did happen. He had prepared a comprehensive plan to share the vision for expanding his division. He presented it to the executive committee, which included Leonard. Leonard ridiculed him, poked holes in his presentation, and caused him to leave the meeting feeling totally humiliated. Bill later told a friend that he couldn't go on anymore. This had happened numerous times before, and even the other VPs were afraid of Leonard. Bill's parting words as he left the company and his career were, "I'd rather quit than face Leonard the Hun and his humiliating criticism another time." What a satisfying victory—the living equivalent of a corporate poison pill.

But work is not the only place Leonard has been able to use his gift, Flambeau. He's also found a way to employ it among the Competition's congregation. When he was elected to the Competition Unit board, he executed a masterful ploy during their budget discussions. First, he goaded Marshall, who has a particular weakness for what they call missions, into proposing a 20 percent across-the-board increase in their giving to further the Competition's strategic plan in distant lands. That certainly looked like a defeat for us, and it would have been if it had been adopted. But when the entire budget was presented, Leonard chose the opportunity to demonstrate his own financial astuteness. He carefully and elaborately explained how the Competition Unit just couldn't afford any increase. In fact, by the time he had finished underscoring the financial problems faced by our Competitor's Glencrest branch, the board actually decided to trim what they call their missions budget by 10 percent. And he managed to make Marshall look like a fool in the process. It was a good evening's work.

As you can see, Flambeau, this is precisely the way we like to see this gift of criticism operate. Leonard actually accomplished three objectives:

1. He hindered the work of the Competition.
2. He managed to put down another of the Competition's clients by heaping humiliation and shame on him.
3. He was able to follow the example of our Chairman Below by exalting himself.

By the way, Flambeau, never forget that self-exaltation is an integral part of each of these gifts I'll be telling you about.

It was our Pernicious CEO's ultimate act of defiance against the Competition; it's what they inaccurately like to call "the Fall," although we refer to it as the original assertion of self. We always want to motivate our clients to act like our Enterprising Founder. They simply must exhibit as much pride as possible; and if they can do so at the expense of another, all the better.

It would be helpful for you to be aware that some people in the Bible supposedly were among our Competitor's White Knights, but they used this gift well. Pointing out this fact can motivate those who think they are serious students of the Competition's Business Plan to become more effective in furthering our corporate interests.

As we analyzed our Competitor's assets, we recognized three people who played key roles in leading the Competition's people out of Egypt under their Previous Business Plan (PBP). At first, it seemed as though both Aaron and Miriam would follow the Competition as effectively as had Moses, their leader. After all, Miriam led a coordinated effort to extol the Head Competitor, and Aaron served as the Competitor's chief ritual functionary (the "high priest" equivalent of our own exalted low priest).[1]

But when the Israelites camped at a place called Hazeroth, both Miriam and Aaron criticized Moses because he had married an Ethiopian woman. That, my young Flambeau, was a masterful strategy, and it works just as well today! Pick out someone who's having an effective role in helping the Competition's cause, look for an area of weakness—especially within that person's family—and then blast away with both barrels! Corporate officers or "ministers" of the Competition are especially susceptible to having their families criticized. I know of a number of their LCU managers who have quit our Competitor's service because of criticism of their families. One man, in particular, left his congregation and his wife after being subjected to a barrage of criticism. Today he proudly serves our CEO Below as the manager of a casino—certainly a far more effective use of his talents than administering one of our Competition's outposts!

Flambeau, if you've ever watched the sport of boxing—one of the finest sporting activities among humans—you know the value of a one-two punch. Miriam and Aaron utilized this approach with effective results.[2] The man whose work for the Competition they sought to undermine, Moses, was said to be very humble. That's one of the vices we have to work hardest to counter. But he had demonstrated a propensity for anger that our people were able to use to counter his humility and his reliance on the Competition. Miriam and Aaron attacked Moses' humility head-on when they said, "Has the Lord indeed spoken only through Moses? Has he not spoken through us also?"[3] Their assault was so effective it even captured the attention of the Competition and forced him to intervene.

I recall a case from an assignment very similar to yours that I was given at a Competition Unit in another part of the country. It involved the son of a "pastor" (that's a term the Competition picked up from the regrettably dead Latin language meaning "sheep manager") and his Sunday instructor. The teacher's name was Helen, and the young man, Arthur, was what humans refer to as hyperactive. (It's a biochemical disorder that affects these humans, and it's a tool our firm can occasionally use to further our cause.) Anyway, this particular problem made it difficult for the young man to sit still and pay attention. Since I was assigned to young Arthur, I was able to cash in on his distractibility to create chaos both in the Christian school he attended and in his Sunday instruction class.

Now disrupting things is pretty normal for nine-year-olds like Arthur. However, I employed another strategy, one you would do well to remember and emulate, Flambeau. I began to plant and cultivate in Helen's mind thoughts such as, "Arthur is the pastor's son; he shouldn't be this way. If the pastor had been doing the right kind of job as a father, Arthur wouldn't have problems like this. In all likelihood, since Arthur is so distractible and tends to misbehave in Sunday school, that's a pretty good indication that his father and mother are lousy parents. They probably shouldn't even be in ministry."

After cultivating these thoughts for some time, I impressed on Helen the importance of verbalizing this criticism to as many people in her Competition Unit as possible. The result, Flambeau, was outstanding. I was able to coordinate my tactics with other members of our team assigned to this outpost of the Competition. Before long, the LCU manager's wife became so upset with Helen's criticism that she came very close to forcing her husband to quit. Also, by bringing Helen's criticism out into the open, I was able to reverse a period of sustained growth, during which quite a few clients had been added to the Competition's rolls. Our strategy motivated a number of the more vulnerable members of their group to quit attending the Competition Unit altogether! It was one of my outstanding triumphs, and the gift of criticism played a large role.

Sometimes it's most effective to motivate the LCU manager himself to exercise the gift. I recall a Competition Unit in which a colleague of mine was able to influence a client we'll call Robert, an experienced and successful LCU manager, by encouraging in him an attitude of pride—that virtue our Infernal Founder and CEO has so admirably exhibited—and a spirit of bitterness toward individuals who failed to show respect for his opinions. My colleague taught this LCU manager to time his criticisms. He learned to level them just when a word of encouragement might have motivated his people to raise their service to the Competition to a higher level. His critical words, of course, turned them in our direction. His fault-finding ability and his four favorite words—"Let me tell you"—helped discourage many of his congregation and even other young LCU managers who sought his advice. One young LCU manager, in particular, became so dismayed that he quit his LCU and became a successful building contractor, using his time, energy, and resources for himself rather than for the Competition.

Let me close, Flambeau, with two or three practical suggestions regarding the tool of criticism. First, whenever Gene or any of your clients attempts to compliment or encourage someone, always remind them of the importance of being balanced. Whenever they try to encourage, ensure that they temper any positive affirmation by pinpointing some weakness in others. Our market research indicates that this approach is most effective in countering their strategy of affirmation.

Second, work on their thinking so they will realize how good it feels to elevate themselves by putting others down. I once suggested to an individual who seemed reluctant to use the gift of criticism that it's a lot like being part of a group of non-swimmers in deep water. The best way to survive is to lift yourself out of the water by pushing others down. It made sense to my client, and he began exercising his gift of criticism more effectively.

Finally, always underscore the value of criticism in your client's thinking. Remember that our Head Guy is also called the Master of Lies, and proudly so. The thoughts you plant don't have to be true—they just need to sound credible. Remind a father, for example, that if his kid has five A's and a B on his report card, he'll be helped most if the father focuses almost exclusively on the B. Instruct members of the Ladies' Group at the Competition Unit that the younger women need to be told that some of the new outfits they wear are tasteless, and that their children are disruptive. Far better that they keep themselves and their noisy brats at home.

I could continue, but I think you get my point, Flambeau. Criticism is one of the most valuable weapons in our corporate arsenal. Hotspur has found it to be a most useful tool, and this has helped fuel his recent rise up the corporate ladder. Don't fail to implement it widely at Glencrest.

>>CONFIDENTIAL MEMO THREE<<

To: flambeau@darkcorp.com
From: scraptus@darkcorp.com
Subject: Effectively Using the Gift of Manipulation

In my previous memo I mentioned Hotspur's recent rise up the corporate ladder. I don't want to mislead you, Flambeau. Young Hotspur is on a fast track, although he lacks your subtle touch. He's like old Slerchus, his mentor, relying too much on frontal assault and not employing sufficiently subtle deceit. Creativity must become the watchword of the day—diabolical creativity, of course! The era of the frontal assault on the Competition has passed. We must be innovative with our clients and, in the process, teach them the clever skills of Our Pernicious Founder. That's why I want you to pay careful attention to what I have to say about the skill of manipulation. It's been around for centuries, but it's become an incredibly useful weapon in our ageless struggle. After all, it was one of Our Debased Chairman's most effective abilities.

You'll want to be sure to utilize a generous dose of manipulation in your efforts to undermine the progress of the Competition and bring your client, Gene, more firmly under your influence. This skill can play a valuable role among the membership of the LCU of Glencrest, and I want to urge you to diligently cultivate its use. It fits the character of our Pernicious CEO extremely well.

Now it's important to understand, Flambeau, that when it comes to the gift of manipulation, motivation is the main issue. Bear with me as I relate an important lesson from history. One of the strongest of our Competition's Takeover

Barons was a corporate leader named Paul, who authored much of their Current Business Plan (CBP). Before this our people had been very successful among the Competition's followers in Corinth (after all, that city had been one of our corporate strongholds for a long time). Then this character Paul established a beachhead among our followers. Although we were able to motivate them to give him a hard time, he experienced a measure of success.

One of his tactics was to use the tool of manipulation, but with the kind of motive we simply cannot countenance. In a directive to the Corinthians, he explained that he was prepared to come to them for a third visit. But, unlike our Chairman and the people of our way, he refused to be a deadweight to them. In contrast to our approach, he claimed that he wasn't after what was theirs, just their welfare.

How ridiculous! Flambeau, always endeavor to railroad your client into taking for himself what belongs to someone else—their property or financial resources, their sexual virtue, their spiritual respect. Remember that manipulation involves influencing a person toward our CEO Below rather than allowing them to go uninfluenced, and always with your own personal gain and interests in mind.

You see, our people in the Competition Unit in Corinth had spread a rumor that this apostle was unscrupulous. (It wasn't true, but, as you know, one of our favorite corporate values is never to allow the truth to restrict us.) We tried to paint a portrait of him in the minds of the Corinthians that parallels some of the successful portraits we've painted of televangelists and others today (it's helpful that those contemporary pictures have their roots in reality). However, this raider Paul refused to exploit the Competition Unit's generosity and divert funds for his own use.

We were able to motivate many of the people in the group at Corinth to figure that, since everybody else looks out for "number one," surely this Paul must have done so as well. We convinced a number of them that collecting funds for the Competition's followers in Jerusalem was simply a convenient way of manipulating them to support him, and that he was just an asset stripper at heart.

Several times in his directive, he used the word for "exploitation," a term that suggests he was employing a devious reverse psychological pressure. We encouraged the people to think that he wanted to appear "godly," since he refused to exercise his right to personal compensation while simultaneously requesting generous financial contributions for this collection he was undertaking, supposedly for altruistic reasons. We almost succeeded in portraying him as a hero from our perspective—as if he were a man of guile and trickery. Unfortunately, we failed because we simply could not divert his motives from what the Competition wanted.

However, as you know, Flambeau, we've now become much more successful in incorporating this strategy into our business plan. One major reason is that we've learned down through the centuries how best to target and influence the motives of others. I don't have to recount for you the examples of some supposed servants of the Competition who've used the airwaves for our purposes. At one point, I was given the assignment of working at an early Competition radio station in a large metropolitan area of the American Southwest. I arranged to have a number of men become a part of the programming lineup—men who were masters of this skill of manipulation. Some of them managed Competition Units, while others simply devoted themselves to their radio efforts and their bodily pleasures and pursuits—which we, of course, encouraged.

I watched with delight each day as one after another of these men pulled into the parking lot in their expensive cars and strolled into the studio wearing the latest, most stylish suits, their hair carefully coifed, and their nails manicured. Then I listened as they delivered a series of gut-wrenching, tear-jerking stories about how they were down to their last dime, their families were destitute, their "ministries" were about to go off the air if they didn't receive a sacrificial gift immediately! Imagine the reaction of some of those impoverished widows who listened! They were so gullible. These guys are heroes in my book, corporate raiders—like the man who succeeded in soliciting millions from his "ministry" when his house collapsed in an earthquake while he concealed the fact that he owned a lavish home in another state. Then there was that outstanding agent who allegedly served our Competition while, in fact, he was scamming and manipulating people. Unfortunately, his long and glorious career was finally brought to an abrupt halt when it was discovered and publicized that he had been cashing contributors' checks while trashing their heavenly wish lists.

But I don't want to give you the wrong idea, Flambeau. The gift of manipulation is not the proprietary property of these media flim-flammers. It can also be utilized among the Competition at the level of their "local churches"—where your assignment is! It's an effective tool you could use to re-acquire control over Gene's activities and motives. Remember, the Competition may have secured his soul, but we can still take over his performance. And manipulation can help subvert even the most sophisticated of the Competition's defense devices. Recently, Philip, the owner of a service business and a prominent member and teacher within the congregation of your charges, told one of his employees, a relatively new follower of the Competition's way, "Dale, we love you unconditionally—just keep performing on the job."

Now, just having him make that statement wasn't the whole story, Flambeau. Philip had to follow up with an occasional comment about Dale's lack of skill or dedication, which he seemed to relish doing. Those frequent comments motivated Dale to give up time with his family to spend longer hours at work, which, in turn, helped Philip earn more money. From our perspective, that's a win-win situation! Philip became increasingly materialistic while Dale spent fewer hours with his family to earn the approval of his boss. Flambeau, you need to look for such situations and maneuver your clients toward them every chance you get.

Let me explain another way this gift of manipulation can aid our struggle for control. Terry was a young, relatively inexperienced LCU manager of one of the Competition's branch offices in a small town. When there were some conflicts, our agents prompted several people within the group to announce their intention to quit. Terry actually considered quitting too, but, like many of the Competition's staff, he chose to persevere. However, he made one fatal mistake. He mentioned his discouragement to Joe, one of our clients. Using his gift of manipulation to greatest advantage, Joe asked Terry if he had ever considered leaving. When the naïve young fool admitted he had, Joe nailed him.

"Then you can't continue working in this church. The only ethical thing for you to do is to speak up in the next business meeting. Be honest about things, Terry. Tell them you're thinking of leaving."

Flambeau, it was a masterful stroke. Young Terry, falsely believing honesty to be the best policy, did just that. Thinking the Competition Unit leadership would accept his concerns at face value, he voiced them, including his thoughts about the possibility of leaving. In doing so, he left himself completely vulnerable.

His comments set the stage for Joe to speak up and demand, with the agreement of the others, that Terry go ahead and resign immediately. In the process, Joe succeeded in reducing the so-called "spiritual" leadership of that Competition Unit by 50 percent and discouraged a potentially effective servant of the Competition's cause.

Of course there are other effective ways to employ this crafty gift of manipulation, and you must be aware of all its varied uses. Gerald was one of the slickest human manipulators I've ever known. One of our followers to the hilt, a true corporate raider in the mold of the shrewdest in human business, he inserted himself into the "concerned core" of a Competition Unit under my assignment, and began dating a woman who had recently experienced a painful divorce. Gerald demonstrated a willingness to listen and voiced a great deal of what I've laughingly referred to as "spiritual concern." In reality, Gerald's concern was to further his own desires by taking advantage of Laura sexually—and that's exactly what he did! First, he won her heart, then he convinced her to surrender her virtue.

The way he did it was utterly devilish, Flambeau! He chose the ideal strategy for circumventing her defenses. First they would read the Bible together, usually with Gerald making pious-sounding comments, then he would place his arms around her and lead the two of them in prayer. Before long, he had manipulated her to the point where their "devotional" times would end in sexual intimacy. Both our Infernal Founder and Calamdus were delighted. They thought it was a wonderful tactic! Needless to say, the woman had been manipulated into a place where she was overcome with guilt and shame and was hindered from effectively serving the Competition.

Incidentally, one of my heroes from their Previous Business Plan is a man who began as an executive of the Competition but wound up consulting one of our personal communication practitioners. Saul, their first manager (they referred to them as "kings"), became a master at manipulation. You may recall how the Competition's lead forecaster, Samuel, anointed a young man named David to take Saul's place. Then when David killed a giant in battle and gave the Competition credit, everyone in Israel began singing the young man's praises. Our man Saul become furious and jealously sought to put David to death. When Saul was unable to pin the young man to the wall with his javelin, one of our representatives whispered a brilliant suggestion into his ear. "King Saul said to David, 'Here is my older daughter Merab; I will give her to you as a wife. Only be valiant for me, and fight the Lord's battles.' For Saul thought, 'Let my hand not be against him, but let the hands of the Philistines be against him.'"[1]

It was another stroke of brilliance on Saul's part: Use the idea of fighting the Competition's battles—a matter of clear interest to this enemy David—as a way to have him put to death! We always believe in attempting to use what the Competition considers another person's strength to trip him up. You'd be surprised, Flambeau, how effective this tactic can be.

Unfortunately, it didn't work in this instance, because

somehow David fell under the Competition's protection and killed those who should have taken his life.

However, you may recall that later in his life, we actually experienced a measure of success against David. We caught him at a vulnerable point, a mid-life crisis, as these humans refer to it. One of our agents suggested to him that he take time off during a battle against Jordan and stay home. We then arranged for him to spot a beautiful woman bathing in the courtyard next to his palace.

Since David was king, he had the authority to invite the woman to his palace, and there they consummated the affair. That delighted the Top Guy Down Below, because David had been called a man after the Competition's heart. But then we achieved another milestone. When the woman became pregnant, our agent helped David develop a plan to manipulate her husband, Uriah, so that David's tryst would be covered up. Now Uriah had been one our clients, a Hittite, until David influenced him to merge with the Competition. Imagine the delight of our Chairman when David attempted to get Uriah to come home and spend the night with his wife.

When those efforts failed, David carried out what we consider one of our crowning achievements. He sent a directive back with Uriah to his captain, Joab. The directive contained instructions to maneuver Uriah into a place where he would be killed in battle. Although Joab worked for one of the Competition's corporate officers, he was a man who typically followed our agenda. He implemented the orders perfectly; the result was Uriah's death. It was one of the most successful cover-ups we've ever engineered!

Now don't get the wrong idea, Flambeau. Most manipulation doesn't lead to someone's death, although we're certainly delighted when it does. Usually, it simply undermines confidence in another person, causing bitterness and disenchantment, and, most important of all, furthers our Debased Leader's agenda of deceit.

In closing, let me share with you two or three areas of concern, things you need to keep in mind when you seek to motivate your clients to use manipulation.

First, ensure that they're aware of one of our CEO's most important maxims: The end always justifies the means. If you can get them to rationalize this way, they'll be far more effective at manipulation. As one of the Competition's LCU managers used to put it (he was particularly effective at manipulating people to respond to his "invitations"), "It's for their own good—and even if they don't have a clue what they're doing, at least the large number of decisions will appear to be a spiritual victory." I don't think the guy ever realized how his deeds aided our corporate strategy while putting feathers in his own cap.

Second, always remember that manipulation and deceit go hand in hand. One of the Competition's favorite maxims is "speak the truth in love." This effort must be hindered at all costs if manipulation is to succeed. You need to do everything in your power to disrupt anyone who attempts lovingly to speak the truth. You can do this in a couple of ways. One is to help people see things in shades of gray rather than in black and white. That's always a helpful strategy according to our CEO Below. Another way is to let them speak the plain, unvarnished truth but harshly so it simply cannot be swallowed. Have them take the sugar coating off the pill and force it down the nearest throat without any liquid, Flambeau. That approach always works well.

Finally, remember that the best example of manipulation

can be found in the early career of our Enterprising Founder himself. Remember when, disguised as a reptile, he instituted our original takeover by offering that first woman the forbidden fruit? "You'll be like God," he cleverly suggested, "knowing good and evil. Besides, God just wants to keep something good from you." But he didn't stop there. "Furthermore," he insinuated, "God was lying to you when he said you would die if you ate that fruit. He just doesn't want you to know what he knows."[2]

It was our Boss's crowning moment to date. In fact, the combination of his distortion of the Competition's words and his subtle reminder of how desirable the fruit was prompted the woman and her husband to eat. It was the first effective case of greenmail! As you can see, Flambeau, manipulation is perhaps the original of our Pernicious CEO's gifts—and one we need to bestow lavishly on our clients today.

I've certainly been impressed with how effectively Hotspur has acquired and distributed this skill among his clients. Given your advanced level of experience with our firm, I'm expecting even more from you.

>>CONFIDENTIAL MEMO FOUR<<

To: flambeau@darkcorp.com
From: scraptus@darkcorp.com
Subject: Communication Our Style—Gossip

As you know from your experience, our human clients have made communication a major priority. Their technology has given them outstanding means for achieving this end. We have found this technology—cellular telephones, digital pagers, portable laptop computers, and, of course, the Internet—to be extremely useful in our Revised Business Plan.

For many centuries now, however, we have been able to challenge the Competition effectively with a communication strategy that seems to work with more rapidity than even the latest human technology.

I'm referring to what our rivals have given the archaic label "gossip." The outdated language in their revered "Scripture" often identified those who engage in such activity as "tale-bearers." I'm sure that many individuals within the group at the LCU of Glencrest possess the necessary curiosity, skills, and attitude to employ this important tactic. As you work with Gene and the others who are under your care, you must be sure to cultivate the skill of gossip.

Flambeau, one of the greatest hindrances to fulfilling our agenda among the Competition's people is a certain reticence on the part of many of them to spread rumors. As our Enterprising Founder has frequently told us, every human has something of which he or she can be accused, and the more widespread and varied the accusations, the greater the benefit to our strategic initiative.

So you'll appreciate the value of the gift I'm discussing, don't forget the words of Peter, that wretched leader in the early CBP days, who warned the Competition's followers not to let anyone suffer as a murderer, a thief, an evildoer, or a busybody in other people's matters.[1] You may think that being a busybody or a gossip is a relatively unimportant vice, but, according to the Competition, it can rank right up there with theft, murder, and other positive forms of evil.

As you consider Gene and other clients among the LCU of Glencrest who might qualify for your special assistance in developing this gift, here are some suggested qualities to look out for:

1. curiosity
2. persistence
3. a willingness to play fast and loose with the facts
4. an unguarded tongue

The first of these qualities, a curiosity about secrets, is fairly common among humans. After all, their most noble art forms—exposé television programming and sensationalized tabloid newspapers—deal in supposed secrets about the rich and famous among them. All you have to do is simply stir up the natural curiosity of those who follow our Competition, and they'll follow right along with the rest.

After all, according to one of the Competition's supposedly wisest followers, the key activity of a tale-bearer is to reveal secrets.[2] The implications are clear: The more dirt on each other these followers of our Rival dig up and the more widely they spread it, the less effectively they follow the Competition's instructions to love each other and the better our cause is served. It shouldn't take a demonic genius to figure this out, Flambeau.

Years ago, during my tenure at a Competition Unit in another part of your region, I targeted a young accountant named Jerry, one of the Competition's most diligent followers. He had just been elected to the Competition Unit board and was curious to learn more about what the Competition had written in that most dangerous of books they encourage each other to study. Let me explain how I used Jerry's curiosity to divert him and get the better of him.

I had him stumble across the fact that several people in his congregation had secrets. He discovered that a fellow board member, Alan, a man much older and more experienced in the so-called faith than himself, had a problem with alcohol. The man never became drunk in public; in fact, no one but his wife and immediate family knew what was going on—until Jerry found out! I had Jerry gain initial leverage by faking genuine concern for Alan and his problem. Then I whispered into his mind that the "Christian" thing to do was not to let Alan get away with this kind of secret behavior. The Competition might have told him the same thing, but our strategy is much more effective than their so-called loving confrontations, which keep problems at the level where they can be handled. Our goal is much more like the bulldozer approach—spread the dirt as far and as wide as possible!

When Jerry discovered how much fun it was to spread this story and how many people rejoiced in hearing "the scoop" on Alan, he was hooked! Before long, he had abandoned his efforts to study that Book, choosing instead to concentrate on digging up every potential scandal he could and spreading it as widely as possible. After all, where there's a void in communication, conjecture grows. And conjecture generally takes a negative turn.

A quality essential for successful gossips is persistence. It's not enough simply to wonder if the Competition Unit music director is carrying on an affair with the lead soprano in the choir, or if one of the deacon's daughters had an abortion a decade earlier. Successful gossips have to break through the resistance of the so-called faithful spirits who try to conceal such things. That's where persistence enters the picture. After all, inquiring minds need to know!

The telephone is a marvelous invention. At times I think it's been more useful to our Infernal Boss than any other modern technological tool. In an earlier era, as you recall, people had to travel from house to house. In fact, as that miserable raider Paul wrote to the young man he mentored, Timothy I think his name was, that's how gossip was carried on in the days of our Competition's firsts followers. Paul warned Timothy about this, explaining that many younger widows would put their own personal desires above the Competition, begin to cast off their original faith, and cultivate the desirable habit of wandering idly from home to home, exercising the gift of gossip, saying things the Competition didn't want them to say, and furthering our causes.[3] Just think how much time was wasted by their lack of technology. After all, it took much longer in those days for a client to visit a dozen households to spread a spicy story than for one of yours in Glencrest to pick up her telephone, use the preprogrammed speed dialer, and divulge some juicy details to a dozen of her closest "friends." And that's not even factoring in e-mail, Internet chatrooms, or the cellular phone!

Incidentally, we've found that men are now just as capable

of carrying out this activity as women. Perhaps it's equal opportunity. Jerry had to place only one call to any of three people to get a story going. Frequently, when he dug up some dirt, he phoned Lois, supposedly to talk with her husband, Bob, who served with Jerry on the finance committee. Just a hint to Lois, and Jerry could ensure the telephone lines would be buzzing throughout the Competition Unit.

In addition to persistence and curiosity, those who exercise the gift of gossip must be willing to play fast and loose with the truth. I must reluctantly agree with the author of the Competition's proverbs when he contrasted a tale-bearer with a person of a faithful spirit.[4] Anything we can do to undermine trust—including distorting the facts, stretching the truth, or telling outright lies—is useful to our strategic takeover objective.

I must tell you a story of how we nearly brought down the career of a gifted young LCU manager named Warren. He had been involved in a counseling situation with a young lady. Tracy, the wife of one of his board members, happened to discover the two of them leaving the Competition Unit office together one day just after dark.

Now Tracy is one of those people who tends to believe the worst about everyone and everything (another helpful tendency for those who engage in the noble sport of gossip). When she spotted Warren placing an arm on Cindy's shoulder, Tracy put nothing and nothing together and came up with scandal. Before she was finished, she had called fifteen of her friends, asking each of them to guard carefully what she was about to tell them (this ploy usually guarantees a widespread distribution of the story) and informing them she was "99 percent sure" that Warren was having an affair with Cindy. She gave further credence to her story by affirming that she had seen the evidence herself; her concerns were not based on hearsay or the gossip of others.

We danced with glee when the Competition Unit counsel rushed into action due to Tracy's gossip and the influential role her wealthy husband played in the Competition Unit. Of course, most of the Competition Unit assumed the old adage that "where there's smoke, there's fire." Although nothing was proven, since there had been no affair, Warren, the LCU manager, was forced to resign in disgrace. As an added bonus, Warren's marriage was strained to the breaking point, and his wife wound up quitting the Competition Unit and becoming bitter toward "those hypocritical Christians." It was a most effective ploy!

Never forget, Flambeau, that to our CEO Below untruth is like salt. It adds taste to just about anything. Consider using this approach early and often among your charges at the LCU of Glencrest.

This brings me to a fourth and final skill that can contribute to effective gossip: an unguarded tongue. Charlie and Lucille were among my earlier clients and had served the Competition on what they call a "mission field" for a number of years. Supposedly they were among the Competition's most effective and talented executives. I tried several tactics to enlist them, all without success.

Then one day, as I listened in on a conversation following a Competition Unit meeting, I realized that I'd been overlooking the obvious. They were sitting around the table discussing their suspicions about a fellow missionary who was their team leader and the man to whom they were responsible. I was able to zero in on their discontent with this man, focus their curiosity on some apparent irregularities in the team's finances, and then let nature take its course.

When they came back to their home country to visit supporting churches, I gently suggested that they voice their suspicions to several of the LCU managers and to the recruitment committee chairmen. At my insistence, they did so while always pointing out that they were simply sharing their concerns confidentially and as a matter for prayer. (Taking that approach sounds so much like the Competition!) Several times they repeated phrases such as "I'd never speak of this with anyone else, but I feel especially close to you," and "I know you share our concerns that the work be done in the right way."

To our delight, shortly after they returned to the field, several of those supporting units decided to pull the plug on their support—so it was a form of "reverse greenmail." Their team leader resigned, they were placed in charge, and a work that had been extremely effective for the Competition has now become one of our more successful outposts.

From what I've told you, Flambeau, I'm sure you can identify the benefits of the gift of gossip, or tale-bearing. For your enlightenment, however, let me review several of them.

First, gossip violates the Competition's law. You may recall that when our Chief Competitor gave his first set of business directives to his former Egyptian branch manager, Moses, he included a statement that they were not to "go about as a tale-bearer" among the people.[5] For that reason alone, it would be worthwhile cultivating more tale-bearers.

But there are other benefits as well. As you have seen from the accounts I've shared with you, gossip reveals secrets. Those who gossip love to dig up the dirt and scatter it around. The more that happens, the more the strategy of the Competition is hindered, and the more effectively our business plan can be carried out.

A third benefit is that gossip generates strife. It's like fuel to a fire; in fact, that miserable king who wrote the proverbs in the PBP pointed out that, just as the absence of wood causes a fire to go out, so the lack of gossip will bring strife to an end.[6] That's why it's important to keep the fires stoked by ensuring that your target congregation always has a good mixture of gossip and choice morsels to spread. Perhaps Gene himself could become a gossip; if not, that woman who pirated him into the Competition's camp might prove to be a worthy candidate.

Finally, gossip tastes good to everyone who samples it, and, once sampled, it's absorbed into the inner being of both the person who spreads it and the one who hears it. Twice in their proverbs the Competition's writer admitted that the words of a tale-bearer are like tasty trifles that go down into the innermost body.[7] Flambeau, this extraordinary tool very much resembles the sugar-coated pills distributed by human physicians. It tastes great, and it gets into the system quickly. For all these reasons, I urge you to make ample and frequent use of the skill of gossip. You had best take note that Hotspur has often availed himself of this resource. He's had to work hard to overcome the reluctance of those who mentored him to use such contemporary tools. I'm convinced that he, you, and anyone else who wants to taste success in our field of endeavor must employ the fine art of gossip.

In my next memo, I'll have more to say about that extraordinary tool of ours, the human tongue. Just remember—gossip can be one of the most effective vices we can encourage the Competition's people to use. Don't skimp on it.

>>CONFIDENTIAL MEMO FIVE<<

To: flambeau@darkcorp.com
From: scraptus@darkcorp.com
Subject: Expanding Our Effective Use of Human Conversation (The Gift of Gab)

In my previous memo I explained one use for that marvelous piece of equipment uniquely suited to our corporate objectives. I'm speaking, of course, of the human tongue.

I recall a meeting several centuries ago in which my manager, Calamdus, expressed his surprise that the Competition had not ordered the removal of all human tongues. That meeting was one of our most beneficial management conferences because we developed strategies for using this human appendage for our Debased Founder's most vital purposes. After all, the Competition leader named James was correct when he wrote that the tongue can be used either way, to praise our Foe or curse others.[1] The danger this tool poses to our Competitor's agenda is reflected in the statement that anyone who does not stumble in using the tongue will be able to exercise self-control and serve the Competition's cause. We must provide opportunities for stumbling. And the value to us is evident from the fact that the tongue, although a small member of the humans' bodies, has great potential for influence. Like the rudders on ships and planes, it can influence the direction of much larger things. Furthermore, like a small spark, it can generate a huge fire, producing great heat, misery, and destruction, all of which originate in the very office of The Top Guy Down Below.

For that reason, Flambeau, it is imperative that you assist your clients such as Gene and others at the LCU of Glencrest in cultivating the ability to use their tongues properly—that is, to avoid employing them to praise our Competitor and to use them instead to further our agenda.

In this memo I will suggest one way we must prevent our clients from using their tongues if they are to cultivate what I am calling the gift of gab. This will be followed by an extensive examination of the products that can be generated by the appropriate use of the tongue in the manner our Chairman Below desires.

First, however, let me establish the most important premise regarding the gift of gab. Flambeau, it is absolutely essential that we keep these followers of our Chief Competitor from controlling their tongues. After all, the member of the Competition management I mentioned, James, warned those early followers of the Competition that an unbridled tongue leads to useless religion.[2] That's why it's important that we urge these poor human clients to cast off any restraints on what they say. We don't even mind if they speak "religiously" as long as their religion is pointless. In fact, our Perverse Founder delights in religious activity because it usually furthers his agenda more effectively than confrontation or outright opposition to the Competition.

I've referred to our clients' increased use of the media, especially television and radio. These tools have been in existence for only a few short decades now, but it is incredible how effectively we have been able to adapt them to our purposes—often with the willing cooperation of some who claim to be the Competition's most ardent followers. Truly it's the wave of the future!

In an earlier memo I mentioned my first assignment over

this medium in a major metropolitan area in the American Southwest. Although a few humble and authentic agents of the Competition used the airwaves, I succeeded in cultivating a corps of individuals who were far less concerned about what they had to say than about using their words for personal gain. They provided a clever counterfeit of the Competition's forecaster Isaiah, who claimed that he had been given "the tongue of the learned" that he might speak a word in season to those who were weary (we'd certainly give them a tongue lashing, given a choice!).[3] The individuals I recruited for this media task force were, to a man, glib of tongue and fully able to move the hearts of most who heard them. They perfectly fit the profile of the character James talks about. Considering themselves religious, they refused to bridle their tongues, and they deceived their own hearts into thinking that they were helping others. Yet what they were doing was designed to further their own personal prestige and finances. Thus, although the Competition considered their religion useless, it was of great value to our own takeover strategies!

Please note how perfectly such types play into our strategy to convince humans of the value of sincerity, even when it's void of their noxious sense of integrity. We'll have to discuss this in relation to their political figures at another time.

But be careful, Flambeau, not to limit this gift of gab to televangelists or radio preachers who further our cause by pious-sounding appeals, camouflaged concern, and outright chicanery. The more you work with your clients in Glencrest, the more you will discover this skill can be utilized effectively in your overall marketing plan.

Your agenda will be to encourage these fools to pour foolishness out of their mouths, instead of using their knowledge of the Competition wisely, as the writer of Proverbs suggested.[4] You must manipulate them into refusing to guard their ways or restrain their mouths, as the Competition's executive David sought to do.[5] Instead, you will want to expose them to the exhilarating benefits and pleasures of an untamed tongue.

Of course the most effective use of the tongue, and the one that most perfectly fits our Pernicious Founder's nature, is deceit. I'll have much more to say about this in a later memo. Because this is the skill most clearly exhibited by our CEO Below, I think it deserves specific consideration. However, let me simply state here that the Competition ranks a lying tongue near the top of his list of things he despises.[6] That's why it is imperative that, as you work with Gene and the other members of the LCU at Glencrest, you have them employ deceit at every turn. As you know from studying his profile, Gene was an accomplished liar during his military days. Just because he has enlisted in the Competition's service doesn't mean that this skill cannot be resurrected. Remember, Flambeau, he must use it or lose it. And it's your job to ensure that his ability to equivocate and prevaricate is strengthened by frequent use. If our clients can whip their flabby bodies into shape by exercising on those weird contraptions they employ, the least we can do is help them exercise things that can really be of help—such as deceit.

A second valuable use of the gift of gab, and one closely related to deceit, is flattery. In one sense, it's a form of deceit, although it can involve the truth. But the important issue isn't whether flattery is true or false but rather the pride it tends to generate in the human who receives it.

Case in point: Some time ago, one of my clients named

Mel, a gifted singer, was asked to solo for the first time with the Competition Unit choir. I considered giving him a sore throat or a bad case of nerves. Then I thought of a better option, one I had learned about during a consultation with Calamdus, no mean flatterer in his day.

I enlisted five humans and arranged for each of them to lavish praise on Mel after he sang. I had all of them compare him favorably with other soloists. Two of them went so far as to tell him he was "the best they'd ever heard."

Even though he had sung effectively and brought praise to our Chief Competitor, I ultimately succeeded in reversing the damage because all those compliments produced an inordinate pride in Mel's heart. That, in turn, led to arrogance and disdain for others with whom he sang. By the next time he was invited to solo, his entire motivation had been transformed by pride.

But the crowning blow came over a period of time as a result of Sherrie, one of my most skilled flatterers and another member of the choir. Realizing her skill at seduction—a gift I'll discuss in a later memo—I encouraged her to continue using her tongue to flatter Mel. It was like pouring gasoline on a flame. It happened just like their proverbs warn. Sherrie and Mel became sexually involved and, soon enough, neither of them was in a position to sing for the Competition again![7] So you see, Flambeau, the gift of gab can lead to all kinds of positive by-products.

Another effective use of this human skill involves discrediting the Competition by attacking others among the Competition Unit congregation. This has worked in many so-called churches down through the centuries, and it can certainly prove profitable in Glencrest. The Competition uses all kinds of terms to describe this kind of activity: backbiting;

reproaching; speaking like a sharp razor, spear, arrow, or sword; and speaking spitefully. The humans have a saying that sticks and stones may break their bones, but words will never harm them. Don't believe a word of it! More damage can be done with a well-chosen word than with a carefully thrown rock or even a bullet!

Consider an example from Jeremiah, one of the Competition's former chief forecasters. He had been sent to a potter's house (clay pots, you know) to speak to the people of Israel, and he used the occasion to warn those foolish humans to turn from the lifestyle that was so pleasing to our Founder. Jeremiah lamented their refusal to turn from doing things their own way. (We, of course, always pressure humans to "do it their way.") After he warned them that the Competition would judge them, some of my associates whispered in the ears of the leaders of Israel, who then said, "Come, let's devise plans against Jeremiah—it's the only way to stop him. Let's attack him with the tongue and not pay attention to any of his words."[8]

We have used this strategy successfully against the Competition's agents in virtually every generation, Flambeau, and it seems as though these humans derive great enjoyment from it! Somehow they take a perverse delight in attacking the Competition's most effective staff members. Of course our Chairman Below is always pleased when this happens, which could produce an extra bonus for both you and me.

This skill can take so many different forms—sometimes an outright word of opposition, perhaps a veiled barb of criticism, even an appeal to other followers to resist the Competition's LCU managers. The important thing is not how it's done but that our clients use their tongues to attack each other, especially those among them who have chosen to become Competition agents and to target other humans in order to increase their market share.

Several years ago, a small Competition Unit in a rapidly growing neighborhood quite similar to Glencrest had grown under the leadership of a young, enthusiastic leader to the point where the next logical step was to move to a new location and build a new building. Since this marketing strategy enjoyed a great deal of agreement, I chose to focus on one of the older couples in the Competition Unit, founding members they were, too. I impressed on their minds the danger of change, reminded them of the valuable contributions they had made to securing the original location of the Competition Unit, and then gave them ample opportunity to voice these concerns to others. Some people simply refused to listen. On the other hand, quite a number of people heard the barbs willingly, and their enthusiasm for seeing the Competition Unit grow under the leadership of this young LCU manager and for building a new facility vanished like snow in the desert heat. These humans were soon persuaded to voice their concerns to still others, including some of the young, newly persuaded followers of the Competition. Conflict spread like the flu, and instead of constructing a new building, the young LCU manager found himself with half a Competition Unit—and a far less effective beachhead against our corporate endeavors.

Let me give you another example of how effectively the gift of gab can be used. You recall I mentioned Job, the patriarchal object of our Debased Founder's special attentions. The Head Guy wasn't able to get him to curse the Competition and die, although he tried wonderfully persuasive devices. But in his brilliance he came up with an alternate plan.

When the Competition motivated three associates to come alongside Job to encourage him and mourn his losses with him, our CEO waited while they sat silently for seven days.

Then he infiltrated their minds with the thought that the Competition wouldn't allow a series of disasters to happen to Job if he hadn't done something terribly wrong. The rest, as they say, is history! These so-called friends dumped an ocean of verbal venom on Job, who, in turn, responded bitterly toward them and even, at times, toward our Chief Competitor. These results showed how effective it can be for clients to accuse someone of wrongdoing under the guise of encouragement, as our CEO had Job's friends do.

Another effective technique involves the use of a disruptive comment. My former boss, Calamdus, once reminded me of two instances in which some of the Competition's choice followers became disruptive. At one point, when Peter had made a dramatic affirmation of our Chief Competitor's son, our Founder was able to railroad him into trying to dissuade the One he followed from going to Jerusalem to be executed (a major triumph for our side, of course, although not without unexpected developments). Our Chief Competitor actually told him, "Get behind me, Satan." What a delightful response! It's always a coup when we get credit for putting words into an opponent's mouth.

Then there was Martha, who also exercised the gift of control. (I'll tell you more about her in my next memo.) Most of the time, she could be counted on to say something disruptive against our Chief Competitor whenever she was prompted, such as the time she urged him to get her sister to quit listening to him and start helping her with dinner. Or the time she nearly prevented him from raising her brother Lazarus from the dead by pointing out that her brother's body had begun to decay. What she had to say may have been accurate, but her timing was ideally suited to our agenda.

In closing, let me give you a list of uses of the tongue that need to be opposed at all costs. (These are given with references to the Competitor's Current Business Plan so you will be able to counter them.) Remember, Flambeau, our Enterprising Founder didn't hesitate to use the Competitor's writings against him, and you, too, must learn how to do so against your clients.

First, you must prevent them from speaking wisdom or justice. David, who wrote part of their Previous Business Plan, urged them to speak this way, but we simply cannot allow that to happen.[9]

In case you're wondering, from the viewpoint of our Competition, speaking wisdom simply means addressing the situation with the practical life-skills the Competition frequently grants his followers to aid them in pursuing his values rather than ours. Speaking justice is the way our foes attempt to measure every word by the standards of their Business Plan rather than how it suits their personal objectives. Because this is a use of the tongue that promotes human welfare, we simply cannot permit them to speak the Competition's wisdom and justice.[10]

I recall a time when old Slerchus, your former professor, had tried everything in his bag of tricks to subvert one of the Competition's agents. Slerchus threw all the seven deadly "wins" at him—greed, pride, you name it. But nothing seemed to work. When the client was reassigned to me, I brought him into contact with friends at work, who managed to change the direction of his conversation whenever he tried talking about the Competition's values. It took time,

Flambeau, but my strategy worked. The man became less effective for the Competition. Even his physical health declined as a result of my efforts to divert the direction of his conversation.

Second, along that same line of reasoning, they must not be allowed to speak of his Directives.[11] Whenever they begin to discuss that dreadful book, their thoughts and words must somehow be diverted. If nothing else, remind them of some worthwhile yet harmless chore. We must keep that book out of their minds at all costs!

Third, because wise use of the tongue promotes human health, they must not be allowed to communicate the Competition's wisdom. After all, we can't have them healthy, can we? How much better to keep them emotionally disordered and under internal stress. This is one of our most underrated means of unhealth!

Flambeau, it is essential that you recognize the incredible capability of the gift of gab. Our human clients have developed powerful military weapons (wonderful things that come in atomic, hydrogen, laser-guided, and ballistic versions!), yet they have never come up with a weapon with more innate power than the tongue. The Competition's own proverbs recognize that life and death are in its power.[12] I've been keeping tabs on Hotspur's efforts to promote his clients' use of their tongues. He's found a key to career enhancement, and one you will do well to make greater use of yourself. It is vital that we (and you especially) harness this power to further the campaign of our CEO Below. Remember, humans talk about their dog-eat-dog world—they can't imagine our own appetites, can they?

>>CONFIDENTIAL MEMO SIX<<

To: flambeau@darkcorp.com
From: scraptus@darkcorp.com
Subject: The Control Issue

One of those human lowlifes named Acton once stated, "Power tends to corrupt, and absolute power corrupts absolutely." A marvelous salute to the gift of control—really, they can be diabolically astute now and then.

Perhaps in your limited experience, Flambeau, you haven't yet realized how central this issue is to the objectives of our Debased Chief Executive. As you may recall, even the accursed Book of the followers of our Competition reveals that the ultimate objective our Founder Below was to take over the Competition's Corporate headquarters.[1]

Despite a few glitches along the road to this ultimate objective, our Pernicious Boss continues to work vigorously to fulfill this goal, and we must be about his diabolical business as well.

One of the ways we can achieve this goal is by motivating the agents of our Competition to seize control. This is very important, for our Competitor's ultimate goal is to subjugate every being in creation to himself. Submission is his watchword, and it grates upon us like fingernails on a blackboard.

After all, if we don't have control, what do we have? We understand the value of power in corrupting the standards of the Competition. Furthermore, it's like a tonic, a stimulant, to those of us who are part of the management team of our Head Honcho. But it works the same way with our wretched human clients. Many of them just don't realize how much they love to be in charge.

That's why, as you work with Gene and your other clients from the LCU of Glencrest, you will want to utilize the gift of control, one of the key skills from the portfolio of abilities you are motivating them to exercise.

Review your profile on Gene. You'll see from his days in the Marines how important control has been to him. Work to bring out those latent instincts, especially in his relationships with others in the Competition Unit.

Speaking of the Glencrest Competition Unit, let me suggest that you start with those who are already in positions of leadership. You may recall from your required historical studies how successfully we were able to disrupt one of the earliest of the Competition's local agencies through one of their officers.[2] Diotrephes was particularly skilled at exercising this ability. One of my associates, Marphan, had this human as a client. The first thing he did was cultivate Diotrephes's love for the spotlight. We let him see how much fun it was to have others bow and scrape before him and recognize that he was in charge. We allowed him to feel the rush of adrenaline that comes from having others ask, "How high?" when he snapped his fingers for them to jump.

Next, Marphan encouraged Diotrephes to assert himself against other leaders. "What right does John have to write to your church or to visit and to receive acclaim when you are in charge? Where is the local autonomy? Where's the respect for you? Why let someone else challenge your right to lead?"

As a result of cultivating these thoughts, Diotrephes rejected John and other executives of the Competition, preferring instead to seize control for himself.

In addition, Marphan subtly pointed out to Diotrephes the importance of launching a preemptive verbal attack before these other Competition executives could seize control, so he unleashed a blitz of false and nonsensical accusations.[3] As I've so carefully pointed out before, Flambeau, the truth of the accusations isn't the issue; what counts is that they stick—and usually the more outrageous the charge, the more effective the result! Diotrephes was extremely good at using this tactic.

The next step—and an effective one—Marphan encouraged him to take was to formally reject these visiting dignities and to forbid others who wanted to acknowledge them. His final, climatic triumph occurred when he actually had this prominent executive John, who wrote part of the Competition's Current Business Plan, barred from a Competition Unit meeting. What a delightful and triumphant moment it was!

Flambeau, Calamdus has encouraged the use of Diotrephes as a model, and I have employed his tactics successfully in the lives of a number of my clients to thwart Competition takeover strategies in our territory. One of my clients, Tim, was a personable individual with a penchant for taking control and an even greater skill at undermining the control of others. Tim was part of a Competition Unit where the board had become concerned about what the Competition calls "qualifications" for leadership. It took me some time to figure out how to use this to further his skill at acquiring control over others, but when it finally dawned on me, I planted the seeds of thought in his mind. They took root and blossomed successfully.

First, Tim made sure that he was appointed to the church's nominating committee. Then, no matter which names were submitted for leadership, Tim made it a point to investigate thoroughly the lives of each individual with the intent of finding something that would disqualify them.

Eventually, a special session of the Competition Unit board was called, at which Tim presented his findings to the chairman. Before he was finished that evening, Tim had carefully and craftily pointed out some disqualifying flaw in the life of every leader in the Competition Unit, including his fellow board members! I nearly overflowed with glee when the LCU manager finally exploded in anger, interrupting the meeting to point out Tim's own flaws. I just love power struggles, Flambeau; they're an ideal tool in our campaign of harassment.

In another Competition Unit, I was able to experience a significant measure of success with a client named Ted, who was naturally gifted at taking charge. Ted had served as the vice president for a large industrial firm, and he was accustomed to getting his way. When he was converted by the Competition, he carried that attitude with him. I felt we could make effective use of his leadership ability—and we did.

The issue of Ted's leadership role came up almost immediately. When some of the more mature of the Competition's followers suggested that he was a novice and they shouldn't "lay hands on him in ordination" (a revolting ritual of bestowing honorable recognition on a new leader), I prompted Ted to point out his many years of industrial leadership experience and how his skill at building plants and overseeing budgets was just what the Competition Unit needed for their upcoming building program. Needless to say, he was quickly elected, and his power base was secure.

From there, Ted's influence branched out in a number of directions. He was actually able to have two of the church's

LCU managers fired when they tried to bring a more spiritual emphasis to the Competition Unit. Then when a LCU manager came along whose major objective was to build his own power base, I encouraged Ted to work with him and turn the emphasis away from what our Competition calls spiritual priorities to a strategic plan that included building a bigger facility, developing social programs, and assembling a larger congregation than the other churches in the community.

Frequently, Ted would suggest to the LCU managers topics about which they should or shouldn't "preach." He was also careful to censure them when they had "gone overtime" with a "sermon" (a dreadful exercise in inculcating group stupidity).

Flambeau, when you have someone like Ted, with strong abilities, in a Competition Unit, it's easy to get things moving in the direction our Infernal Founder prefers. People like Ted take to power like ducks take to water.

In a later memo I'll discuss the ability to intimidate. It's a related and useful skill; but intimidation isn't the only way to control, and men are not the only humans who can exercise that gift.

You may recall I mentioned in an earlier memo a woman named Martha who played a key role in our Competitor's Current Business Plan. I want to tell you more about her commendable love of control. She had a brother and a sister with whom she lived in a Palestinian suburb called Bethany. Martha was one of those individuals who always wants to take charge. She was especially adept at giving advice; in fact, when the Chief Competitor's son came to visit in their home, and Martha's sister sat down to listen to him, Martha moved into action, pointing out a legitimate problem—her need for help in preparing the meal. She inferred that her guest did not care whether she served without help, and she actually had the audacity to order him to tell her sister to stop sitting there wasting time listening to his platitudes and to come help her with the meal. Although she didn't succeed, she sure stirred things up![4]

On another occasion, Martha's eagerness to give advice and take over a situation almost stopped one of the Competition's miracles in its tracks (our view of these "miracles" is that they are just illusions, a helpful concept to foster in your more modern human types). Her brother had died, and our Chief Rival's son was standing at the tomb. When he ordered those with him to roll away the stone, Martha attempted to use logic to hinder the procedure. She pointed out that her brother had been dead four days and that an offensive odor would be released if the stone were moved. Her willingness to take control almost prevented the Competition from restoring her brother to life.[5]

I recall a client named Laura with whom I worked for a number of years. Laura was given to strong opinions and was not shy about expressing them. She was married to Jason, a member of the Competition Unit board. Now Jason was a wimp who had what the Competition calls humility. I had tried several takeover strategies, pretty much without success, until I figured out that there were a number of tactics Laura could use to lead Jason around by the nose. She could verbally intimidate him, sexually manipulate him, and just outright make his life miserable—and she did it all! Through her ability to control him, she was able to become more influential than anyone on the Competition Unit board.

On several occasions (e.g., when they were considering a new marketing strategy they call "evangelism") Laura was able to raise—through Jason—issues that kept those programs from being implemented. On another occasion, she went straight to the LCU manager to voice her opposition to taking a group of the Competition Unit young people on a short-term overseas marketing and recruitment trip. She raised such a stir about the hazards of travel in Third World countries that, although he didn't want to, the LCU manager was forced to stop the effort. We were very pleased when the young people spent a weekend at an amusement park (a frivolous but useful human invention) instead of on some "mission" field learning to serve the Competition's takeover agenda.

And another thing, Flambeau. It's easy to forget when dealing with your clients that money is one of the most effective tools for control. Remember the Competition's so-called "golden rule?" Well, our Despised Founder has come up with a golden rule of his own: Those who have the gold make the rules! Or course, we haven't needed any medium of exchange such as money in our sphere of authority. After all, we all are fully committed to the strategy of our Infernal CEO. (At least we'd better be!) However, these humans love to toss their money around and use it for influence. According to their way of thinking, when you have money, you have control; and if you lose your money, you lose control. That's why it's important to ensure that your clients get their hands on all the wealth they can; in their realm, money is power.

One of my more frustrating moments came when a Competition Unit in which I had several clients was about to sell their property and move to a different location to construct a new building. One of my colleagues also had a client in the Competition Unit, a man who'd been there since the beginning. In fact, he'd been quite a conscientious follower of the Competition and had sold the land for the original building to the Competition Unit at a reasonable price. He had also been faithful in supporting the Competition Unit with his money. My colleague used that angle to get him to influence the Competition Unit against the new building project.

In a meeting, he stood up and expressed how he intended not to "let this young whippersnapper of a pastor get things out of control. I've been a leader here since it started. We wouldn't have the present location if it weren't for me, and I don't think we ought to consider moving anywhere until I say it's time to think about moving. I've been giving a lot of money to this group, and if anybody entertains the notion of moving, I'll pull my money out. You'll see how quickly this thing will fold."

Unfortunately, my colleague's client didn't carry the day. The Competition Unit went ahead with its foolish decision to move, but we created quite a controversy in the process.

Some people exercise their skill of control through rigid bureaucracy and organization. Maurice, the administrative LCU manager of a large Competition Unit in the southern part of our territory, was the newest staff member of a Competition outlet with twelve LCU managers who were served by six secretaries and two administrative assistants. Maurice was hired because Chad, the senior LCU manager (who was, regrettably, a gifted leader, a visionary, and a dynamic "preacher"), needed help with administrative details. I worked very closely with Maurice, helping him draft a plan that would further our interests. First, I convinced him that administration and control were virtually one and the same. If he wanted to be an effective administrator, he would have to seize control of everything. Every teacher's appointment, each fledgling program, all the budgets—everything had to go through him.

Before long, Maurice had every secretary and both administrative assistants answering to him. He stood at the head of the chain of command. No one, including the senior LCU manager, could get anything done without getting his approval. You can imagine how effectively that hindered all the Competition's acquisition and growth strategies!

Ultimately, I was able steer Maurice to exercise control in ways that caused people from the congregation and his managerial colleagues to resent him deeply—a worthwhile exercise, since resentment ranks high on our Debased Founder's list of desirable feelings. I made sure, however, that he kept his focus on the importance of maintaining control. In fact, I convinced him that he would be disobeying the Competition if he relinquished control over even one small facet of his fiefdom. As you can see, Flambeau, a little self-deception can go a long way when it comes to cultivating such an ability.

The gift of control can also work effectively in their many independent marketing groups, what the Competition's followers refer to as "parachurch ministries," one of their newest assets. Let me relate a case in point.

Marvin had served faithfully in an entrepreneurial marketing outfit (a "missionary ministry") almost from its inception. After a few years of successfully fulfilling a number of responsibilities, he became the assistant to the number two man in the organization, the vice president. When the vice president finally retired, Marvin was the natural choice for the job.

Initially, to my chagrin (because he was my client), Marvin carried out his work with a humble and gracious spirit. I puzzled over how to discover his vulnerability. Finally, after talking with one of my colleagues from another territory and reviewing some of Calamdus's old memos on the gift of control, I hit on a strategy. And did it ever work!

I began planting thoughts in Marvin's mind about how things were changing, and how dangerous change was. I loaded his mind with concerns about how all of these "newfangled innovations" were counter to the purposes of the Competition and how dangerous they might be. Of course, the truth was just the opposite, but we never worry about the truth, Flambeau.

Before long, Marvin began using his administrative skills to transfer all of the new and innovative people to places in the organization where they couldn't be of use to the Competition, and where their skills, drives, and objectives would dry up and wither on the vine. Many of them finally became discouraged and quit. Others wound up trying to take on Marvin, and whenever they did, the "power showdown" that resulted always worked to our benefit. Any time we can generate a public conflict or a power struggle, Flambeau, we win.

Marvin always couched his efforts to control things in spiritual terms, convincing those around him that he had the Competition's interests at heart. In fact, I don't think to this day he realizes how helpful he has been to our expansion strategy.

By the way, Flambeau, let me mention a subtle but effective method of having people try to seize control. Just get them to poke their nose in someone else's business. You remember Peter from our Competition's original followers? Once, when our Head Rival's son confronted Peter over his own lack of steadfastness, Peter was able to divert attention by pointing to one of his colleagues, John, and asking, "What shall this man do?" Although Peter was rebuked, he nonetheless established an excellent pattern for diverting attention to others when the Competition challenged him over a perceived weakness.

On another occasion, this same Peter withdrew from contact with a number of the Competition's followers in a place called Antioch. He was afraid of others in power and what they might think of him, so he stopped eating with Gentile employees of the Competition. What's neat is how the rest of the Jewish Christians played the hypocrite with him. Even Barnabas, one of their leaders, was caught up in this show of prejudice.

Flambeau, the significance for you should be obvious. Whenever a client shows any natural leadership skills, always look for additional ways to have him or her use this gift of control. This tactic is especially effective if others tend to follow them.

In closing, let me suggest ten commandments for control. These can be effectively implemented with any of your clients who show an aptitude in this area.

Commandment 1: Never relinquish control. Remind your people that they must always keep their own hand on the rudder and never trust anyone else to steer the ship. A good time to start with them is during their teenage years, when they naturally come to a point where they want to exercise more personal choice and responsibility. Occasionally you'll be able to push them to the point where they can seize control of the family. Anytime the teenagers run the home, it's as effective for our corporate strategy as putting the inmates in charge of the asylum.

Commandment 2: Never compromise. Convince your clients

that compromise is all right for moral issues but never with issues of control. They must always show others who's boss.

Commandment 3: Never discuss. To engage in meaningful dialogue may open the door for compromise. Make sure your clients are on the giving end of any communication, and that they use a commanding tone. Whenever they communicate, be sure that they follow an axiom seldom taught in language or grammar classes in human schools: The imperative mode is always the best for communication. Remember, Flambeau, your clients must always sound confident, give orders, expect others to obey, and never must be dissuaded by "facts" or the opinions of others. When you have the gift of control, you must use it to keep things from getting out of control.

Commandment 4: Never back down. Encourage your clients to take the approach of the man who once told his junior partner, "I've only admitted to being wrong once in my life—that was when I thought I was wrong, but in fact, I was right."

Commandment 5: Never show weakness. The human novelist Charles Dickens's hero, Ebenezer Scrooge, provides a classic example. Early in his career, before his breakdown, he refused to take a day off for that religious nonsense the Competition calls Christmas. To old Ebenezer, taking a day (or even part of day) to focus on relationships rather than on business was a sure sign of weakness. Old Eb even castigated his employees who dared to try to enjoy the holiday. Remember, Flambeau, control and weakness are like oil and water—they never mix.

Commandment 6: Never let the Competition control their lives. Convince them that they're missing something—freedom, right of expression, personal initiative, whatever.

See to it that they seize control of every aspect of their own lives, including money, time, and talents.

Commandment 7: Remember that control and leadership are one and the same. Don't allow any of that weak and senseless tripe the Competition refers to as "servant leadership." Recognize that silliness for what it is, Flambeau—an oxymoron. Instead, encourage your clients to study the "secrets" of their newest crop of immensely wealthy business executives, industry tycoons, and Hollywood celebrities. You'll gain the added benefit of throwing some greed into the mix!

Commandment 8: Remember that a lack of control is always a sign of weakness. One of the best ways to say this is the phrase chosen by a human deodorant advertiser, "Never let them see you sweat." Remind them that they live in a dog-eat-dog society, and the other dogs are just waiting for an opportunity to chew them up. They must never let down their guard by showing a lack of control.

Commandment 9: Remember that knowledge is control and power. Regardless of whether they know it all, they need to give others the impression that they do. Ensure that their communication carries a tone of absolute certainty that leaves others feeling like objects of condescension. If those around them feel confused, inept, and stupid, that's all the better.

Commandment 10: Maintain control by blaming others for failure. Urge them to be constantly on the lookout for scapegoats, so that when things go wrong (and they will) they can shift the blame to someone else. See to it that they are short on patience toward the failures of others, while quick to respond in covering up their own.

You'll be interested to know that Hotspur has adopted these ten strategic initiatives and seems quite adept at using them. The young upstart continues to take major strides in overcoming the plodding influences of Slerchus and those other incompetent tempters who trained him. See that you make generous use of these initiatives in your own practice. Consider applying the spurs to your own efforts, Flambeau.

>>CONFIDENTIAL MEMO SEVEN<<

To: flambeau@darkcorp.com
From: scraptus@darkcorp.com
Subject: Darkening the Emotional Skies Around the Competition's Followers by Using the Gift of Discouragement

We have three levels by which we may hinder our Competitor's agenda: discouragement, opposition, and intimidation. Later, I'll send you memos dealing with the latter two. I'm sure that, being the intelligent demon you are, you'll notice the progression. Just as humans have a variety of nut and bolt sizes, so you'll find it useful to have a variety of tools to use on your clients to slow the progress of the Competition—or even halt it in its tracks.

One of the greatest hazards to our purposes is something the Competition calls joy. It's a quality some humans have that lets them rise above their circumstances. It seems to come from a happy confidence that their CEO is in control of their lives and all the circumstances around them.

Discouragement is one of the greatest tools developed by our Pernicious Founder to help rid the human race of every vestige of joy. In numerous audits it has been rated as perhaps the most useful of all our assets. Some of our agents who have infiltrated the Competition have become uniquely skilled at spreading clouds of gloom and darkness like a storm front wherever they go. Still, we need to make better use of this tool.

You may recall from your studies of our ancient corporate history that we were able to influence a man named

Thomas, a member of the Competition's original band of followers, to use the gift of discouragement. We did so by turning him into a pessimist and a doubter.

Actually, it would be more accurate to say that he had pessimistic and doubting tendencies, which we simply exploited. After all, exploitation is one of our more effective strategies. Seldom does the charge of the Competition's followers that "the devil made me do it" actually ring true. Sometimes it's an executive level demon like one of us, or more usually some managerial demon even farther down the line, who should get the credit. In most cases, we actually don't have to make someone do anything; we just sort of give them a nudge in the direction of their tendencies. That's why it's important to study our clients carefully, identify their weaknesses, and use them to achieve a takeover for our purposes.

That's exactly what a couple of our Fearsome Boss's executives did with Thomas. At one point, when our Rival's son planned to raise that character Lazarus from the dead, he told his followers that he intended to go to Jerusalem. We managed to get Thomas thinking about the danger he and the others faced and convinced him to express his feelings openly, saying, "Let us also go that we may die with him." It was a very pessimistic comment, designed to discourage his colleagues from going. It also contained a note of sarcasm, a subject I'll discuss in a later memo. Mostly, though, it was just designed to be discouraging. Unfortunately, it didn't work as well as we'd hoped.

The night before the crucifixion, Thomas and the other Competition followers were attending a strategy session when our Rival's son said he was going away to prepare a place for them. He told them they knew where he was going and the way to get there. One of our colleagues was able to prompt Thomas to say, "We don't know where You're going, Lord, and how can we know the way?"[1]

What Thomas said at that moment, especially the way he said it, was vintage discouragement at it's best! All of his colleagues were feeling the chill of their leader's impending departure. The Competition's son was doing his best to cheer them, and Thomas used discouragement brilliantly—a frontal assault, like pouring a large bucket of ice water directly over the glowing embers of a fire where chilled humans are trying to warm themselves.

You'll notice that Thomas's strategy was to weave an assertion in with a question to leave his colleagues feeling discouraged. Actually, the men probably did have some idea of where the One they followed was going, but they just didn't have it firmly fixed in their minds. Thomas capitalized on their uncertainty with his disheartening words, then followed up with a question designed to help them see the hopelessness of their situation.

Unfortunately, our Rival's son was too quick for our client. He responded with what has become one of their favorite sayings—but I'll not upset you by quoting it.

After the alleged resurrection, Thomas was the one disciple who continued to discourage the others when they claimed that they had seen the Competition's son risen from the dead. At the prompting of my colleague, Thomas took a very useful tack, one you might encourage Gene and your followers at Glencrest to use. He sounded intensely practical as well as skeptical when he said, "Unless I see in his hands the print of the nails and put my finger into the print of the nails and put my hand in his side, I will not believe." What an outstanding negativist Thomas was! Healthy skepticism, that's what we like to call it; after all, Flambeau, is there any other kind?

Incidentally, this same negative approach can be used most effectively in LCUs today. I've had numerous clients who worked in groups of the Competition's followers just like the one where your responsibilities lie. They developed what I call "wet-blanket" power, the ability to put a chilling damper on just about anything. Let me tell you about some of the most effective tactics they employ.

First, they always call attention to anything negative. If attendance is down, they're quick to point it out. If there's an improvement, they're either silent or have some explanation. But let the offerings drop, the attendance decline, or anything else go wrong, and they're on it like a dog on a bone.

Second, they always make the worst of any situation. I once had a client named Arnold. He was a brilliant man, and he liked to point out facts, a trait I used to sharpen his skills at discouragement.

When a group member became seriously ill with a foot infection, he had to be hospitalized and given intravenous treatment with antibiotics. When Arnold stopped to visit him (an action to which I had been opposed), I came up with a way of turning the situation to our advantage. I reminded Arnold of another man he'd known who had almost died with a similar ailment. There were differences, but we never let details like that prevent us from using a situation for our own purposes, do we? Arnold told this young follower of the Competition about his friend who had almost died with what he referred to as "something just like what you have." It's true the man survived, Arnold finally conceded, but he had to have his foot amputated. You can imagine the fear and discouragement this generated in the mind of Arnold's young friend!

Another effective technique is to have our clients make discouraging comments about any efforts at positive change on the part of the Competition. They can use phrases such as "That just won't work," "We've tried it before," "It would take too much time," "The people are resistant," or (one of my all-time favorites) "But we've never done it that way before." Someone once referred to that last one as the eight last words of the Competition Unit—but they couldn't be the last words because we keep persuading people to say them over and over!

We have also developed some great nonverbal ways to communicate the gift of discouragement. One is the sound humans refer to as a sigh. Another is the gesture of throwing up their hands in hopeless despair. Gestures such as wringing their hands or rubbing their forehead can also help convey discouragement.

Another effective technique for spreading discouragement is to have your client interject a negative note just at the point when things seem to be turning positive. Timing is everything here. Some while ago in one of our Competition's business schools, several faculty members were meeting as a committee to discuss their lack of office space. Several positive comments had been made, and the group was about to draw up a plan to present to the president and the board. We prompted Virginia, one of the faculty members, to say, "There's no sense in taking this report to Dr. Johnson or those people on the board; they've known what we need. They're not going to help us do anything. We might as well forget it."

When one of faculty members said, "Wait a minute. I think we ought to hear this proposal out," Virginia sighed deeply and said, "Well, if you want to waste your time going over something that's doomed to fail . . ."

Finally, I prompted Virginia, when she saw she still wasn't getting her way, to get up out of her seat, sigh dramatically, and walk out of the room mumbling, "What a waste of time; we're never going to get anywhere with this."

It was a delightful occasion. Almost everyone had come to the meeting anticipating a breakthrough in dealing with a long-standing problem. Their expectations had been high. How wonderful to see them leaving with feelings of hopelessness and disappointment, shelving their action plan for the foreseeable future.

Never underestimate the power of negativism, Flambeau. That's why our Chief Competitor instructed his people to think about things that were pure and lofty and noble and of good report and virtuous and praiseworthy, *ad nauseam.* We, on the other hand, must encourage our followers to think about things that are false, ignoble, unjust, impure, ugly, of bad report, related to vices, and worthy of criticism, *ad felicitatem.* That's where we want them to focus their thoughts.

Another effective tool in the arsenal of any human with the gift of discouragement is "comparison." Do you recall from your corporate history studies when the Israelites were attempting to rebuild their house of worship?[2] Our agents had a number of clients within the camp who were particularly skilled at discouraging their friends. They spoke loudly of the former glory of Solomon's temple, and how the new facility they were constructing was, in contrast, as nothing. It forced a direct response from Haggai, one of our Competition's executives, because it weakened Haggai's contemporaries and discouraged them from working.

Another tool our clients used effectively during that time was the old delaying tactic. It's a tool we use frequently. The Competition's agent, Haggai, accurately noted that we were able to get many of our people to say, "The time is not come, the time that Yahweh's house should be built"—even though they had long since finished construction of their own homes.

Flambeau, there are so many ways to utilize discouragement. Remember that when you take a negative approach, you're really taking power over others, tapping into their potential for despair, and causing them to feel helpless under forces beyond their control. And all at once!

Our clients need regular reminders of huge, inflexible bureaucracies that hinder anything they consider worthwhile. They need to see how illness and accident can wreck the most carefully constructed plans. They should be pushed to the point of feeling angry and helpless about the negative realities of any situation. Remember that negative feelings are like a cold virus among humans—they spread easily and are difficult to stop.

Keep in mind that the negativists' motives are not important. They may wish to stamp out the problem as much as anyone else. They just need to think how real and impossible the difficulties are and convey those feelings to their associates in a way that leaves others paralyzed by fear and inertia.

Another effective use of negativism to counter the objectives of the Competition is to let the followers of our Rival see what great strides we have made in their world. The more they appreciate our assets, the more discouraged they become. Make them aware of the progress of our agents in furthering abortions (the "partial birth" procedure is an especially devilish innovation), of the rampant growth of pornography, drugs, graft, and greed, plus the generally immoral behavior of political leaders—especially the hypocrisy of so-called Competition Unit leaders and clergy. Use these facts to help your clients and those around them feel totally out of control so that they will ultimately throw up their hands and do absolutely nothing. In essence, Flambeau, the ultimate goal of discouragement is paralysis. Remember, anytime you can elicit a weak, wimpy, and fearful response to a situation, you have succeeded. After all, discouragement involves just that—removing courage and replacing it with fear. Our CEO Below operates like a roaring lion, striking fear into those he wishes to devour, an admirable (and accurate) image. We ought to follow his example.

One helpful way to move people toward the effective exercise of the gift of discouragement involves bringing about an inward focus. If they aren't moody already, try to direct circumstances so that they will feel "down" most of the time. Let them wear their feelings on their sleeves, become easily hurt, and be given to oversensitivity and quickness to take offense.

Try to ensure that they never wear a cheerful facial expression. After all, the Competition calls that "look" a medicine.[3] If so, then a negative countenance can work like a poison, infecting the minds and lives of others.

One important underlying attitude that should be cultivated in those with the gift of discouragement is an intense self-hatred. Get them to think thoughts such as *What does it matter if I hate myself; everybody else hates me.* Couple that with frequent reminders of how bad things are in their lives. Keep them focused on their four unhappy kids; their critical, superior-minded spouse; their arrogant boss; and their unappreciative colleagues at work. Remind them that, since the people at the Competition Unit don't care about them, neither should they care about themselves. In fact, if you can convince them that our Chief Rival could care less about them, your campaign of harassment will reach peak success.

Finally, encourage them toward even-temperedness. Now, this may sound strange, but I'm talking about an even temperament that's always grouchy. Make sure they cultivate that chip on the shoulder that leaves them vulnerable to attack.

Oh, and I almost forgot, one final tactic those with the gift of discouragement should use—and you may be surprised to learn how effective this can be—is to have them take potshots. Let me tell you how this can work.

Some time ago two men, Will and Harold, worked for a high-tech firm. Both were engineers, and both were in line for a promotion. Will held seniority, but Harold had the amiable personality that often succeeds in securing a promotion. Sure enough, the management spot went to Harold. On his first day in the new position, as he walked through the modular office area past the coffee pot, he couldn't help noticing the whole staff gathered around Will. There was a lot of laughter, and Harold heard the discouraging comment, "Yeah, that's Harold. Ask him what time it is, and he'll take you through all the steps to making a watch."

Taking potshots is a great way to undermine someone else's determination, resolve, and drive. It doesn't really matter what the motivation is, whether anger, vengeance, or just attention-getting. The bottom line is to engage in a covert operation designed to bring the opposition down.

Griping is another useful tool in the arsenal of the person with the gift of discouragement. Some people call it complaining or whining. In fact, Moses, one of the early Competition executives, called it murmuring. Whatever you call it, it's an extremely effective strategy. With his military background, Gene should be well-suited to being a skilled complainer.

Although some humans simply want to pinpoint problems, or get worries out of their system, skilled carpers tend to wallow in the woe of their troubles and concerns. They never offer solutions, only complaints. Such individuals must never be allowed to focus on steps that could be taken to make things right. Instead, you must help them concentrate on what's wrong and why it's catastrophic and terrible. Even something as minor as the temperature at the Glencrest Competition Unit building can help complainers achieve their goals.

Iris had been a stay-at-home mom, effectively raising three children. For years she taught future employee training programs for a LCU in its Sunday and vacation instruction department. But she became one of my most effective clients because she cultivated the gift of griping or complaining. She never voiced anything aloud, but she could mutter under her breath with the best of them at women's meetings and even in all-Competition Unit business meetings. Her whining toward her husband caused him to lose his normally cheerful demeanor and become a sarcastic, bitter person himself. Eventually, because of her attitude, they were forced to leave the Competition Unit, which both decreased their own effectiveness for the Competition and hindered the Competition's efforts.

Actually, whining, murmuring, or complaining is a form of rebellion, something on which our Infernal Founder places a high premium.[4] Whiners never see it that way, Flambeau, but that's exactly what it is. For that matter, we don't care how they see it; the bottom line is that they engage in it. If they make themselves obnoxious to everyone around them, so much the better. They're just that much more effective at spreading discouragement and gloom.

Just like gossips, whiners find their purposes furthered by that marvelous invention, the telephone. They can spread their negative, cynical poison far and wide, creating a cloud of gloom and doom far beyond their physical presence.

The Israelites who murmured, whined, and complained to Moses about everything from bitter water to a lack of meat ultimately stirred up enough of a problem that even their leader became discouraged and exasperated with them—to the point that he disobeyed our Rival and struck a rock when he had been told only to speak to it.

Incidentally, one of the best things about griping and whining is that it's contagious. Like a cold rain, it tends to penetrate and soak into everyone and everything around it. You should do all you can to see to it that your gripers and complainers stay general and don't get too specific. Also, it's imperative to keep them concentrating on the problems rather than looking beyond to solutions.

Furthermore, if they do begin to look at solutions, make sure that they're unrealistic. Have them take an approach like Jack, who said, "This situation at work is hopeless; I'm trying to do the work of three people and so is everyone else."

I don't mean to gloat, Flambeau, but I think this is one skill I've managed to pass along to Hotspur that he didn't pick up in his training under those reactionaries at the business school. It seems that old Slerchus and his cronies never mastered the subtle art of discouragement. Oh, they were fairly efficient at intimidation, but modern times call for modern methods. Discouragement adds a contemporary touch.

Remember the bottom line, Flambeau. The gift of discouragement is designed to rob those who would follow the Competition of both the joy of the present and the courage to face the future. Always remind them how bad things are, and take away their hope of the situation getting better. The end result will be like sand in the cogs of the Competition's corporate machinery. Never underestimate the value of discouragement.

>>CONFIDENTIAL MEMO EIGHT<<

To: flambeau@darkcorp.com
From: scraptus@darkcorp.com
Subject: Implementing Effective Opposition

You've probably noticed how interested humans have become in athletic contests. Baseball, football, basketball, hockey, you name it. We've found ways to use them all to our advantage. Not that there's anything wrong with human athletic contests, unfortunately. But they offer a lot of potential for distraction, which we can utilize to provide what the Competition might consider unprofitable diversification or diversions.

But that's not my point in bringing up the subject of athletic competition, Flambeau. My goal is to help you see the value of building defenses, establishing obstacles, and creating opposition to hinder our Rival's Primary Business Objective. In each of these human sports, most of those who consider themselves fanatics—or fans, as they abbreviate it—love to see the offensive. What most of them fail to recognize is that defensive efforts, what I'm referring to as opposition, bring about the ultimate success. If we are to effectively hinder the Competition's objectives, we must implement a campaign of harassment and opposition.

You may recall that my previous communiqué dealt with the first of a series of three tools, each of which is progressively larger and stronger than its predecessor. Discouragement, the subject of my last memo, is the standard-size tool, while opposition, our present focus, is larger. In my next memo, I'll address the industrial-strength tool of intimidation.

Humans don't really have trouble understanding opposition. Our Pernicious Boss has so influenced the race that even the littlest and most innocent of them know how to throw temper tantrums, scream defiance, and force their parents to drag them kicking and screaming from the toy section of a department store. So they learn opposition early; and they learn it well.

However, part of your mission is to influence Gene and your other clients at Glencrest to use this tool more effectively, for our profit, while undermining the market strategies of our Competition. You may be surprised to learn that one of the best places to find an "all-star" list of gifted opposers is in the Competition's Current Business Plan. One of their chief executives and authors of the plan, Paul, detailed the list in a memo he wrote to Timothy, one of their middle managers.[1] Though he was one of the Competition's chief corporate raiders and a master of creative resistance, Paul nonetheless admitted to being affected by the strategies of opposition employed by three individuals, Phygelus, Hermogenes, and Alexander. In addition, he explained how two of our Infernal Boss's most effective human executives, Jannes and Jambres, provided opposition and resistance to our Rival's strategies during the era of Moses, the Competition's white knight of the Previous Business Plan.

It's basic, Flambeau. Opposition has two primary objectives. One objective is to pull or push something in a different direction; the other is to bring progress to a halt. For example, let's say that the executives the Competition has placed in charge of your Competition Unit at Glencrest decide to implement some kind of raiding strategy designed to deplete our base of influence while increasing their numbers exponentially. At that point you must find some way to either steer that plan in a different direction or bring it to a stop. Similarly, if Gene should decide to take his study of the Competition's Current Business Plan more seriously than the cursory three minutes he currently gives it, you'd need to take similar action. And always remember, Flambeau, one of our important underlying assets is the human tendency toward opposition. It's not that you have to convince them to do something contrary to their nature; you're simply capitalizing on what they'd really like to do.

Phygelus and Hermogenes, two of our corporate assets who were among the rival faction under the influence of Paul in Asia Minor, provide an excellent example of moving themselves and others in a different direction. The rival leader, Paul, had generated significant short-term gains for the Competition when our agents in the area finally figured out a way to hinder the long-term value of his efforts. They convinced Phygelus and Hermogenes that it was not in their best interest to continue following Paul, and the actions of these two prompted all of their colleagues to turn away from him and move in our direction.

Furthermore, Timothy, their middle manager, seemed to have somewhat perfected the art of opposition himself. The words of his mentor Paul indicate that fear had motivated him to pursue a course of passive opposition toward the Competition's objectives.[2] The combination of fear and shame provided just the right amount of sand in the cogs to slow down this man's progress toward our Competition's objectives.

In addition to fear and shame, pride and perfectionism can also promote opposition. This seems to be what Paul had in view in an earlier communiqué to Timothy when he warned the young manager about those who teach otherwise and do not "consent to wholesome words. . . ."[3] Our agents had been able to take over the efforts of some of their teachers, convincing them to move in a different direction from their so-called wholesome doctrine, utilizing personal pride, a perfectionist obsession with disputes and arguments, and even the old tried-and-true motivation of greed. Flambeau, this is one instance in which a careful study of the words of the Competition's Current Business Plan can help you use their warnings to craft opposition in the minds and lives of your clients today.

I must tell you about one of my clients from an earlier assignment, a corporate executive named Max who had been a casualty of one of the earlier takeover wars but who still demonstrated a penchant for opposition. He had risen to a sphere of influence within the Competition's organization when he figured out an unusual and creative way to generate opposition. One of the Competition's favorite seasons is what they refer to as Christmas, when they celebrate the birth of our Rival's son. Among their many useless activities is the singing of what they call Christmas carols. Max had little use for this "emotional nonsense," a label that I suggested and he gladly adopted. Making a great deal over a point he considered consistent with their Current Business Plan, he insisted that one of their favorite carols, "Joy to the World," actually made no valid reference to the birth of the Competition's Chief Baby but in fact referred to another of the Rival's son's appearances. Max did such an effective job arguing his point that the entire "spirit of Christmas," which these Competition Units seem to value so much, was thoroughly undermined. Thus, he fit perfectly Paul's description: "proud, knowing nothing, but obsessed with disputes and arguments over words, from which come envy, strife, reviling, evil suspicions, useless wranglings of men of corrupt minds. . . ." Flambeau, those are the kinds of ingredients we want to introduce into the Competition's body of followers, and talented individuals such as Max can utilize the skill of opposition most effectively.

Jannes and Jambres, two of our heroes during their Previous Business Plan, withstood Moses, one of the Competition's top executives, by providing dramatic but counterfeit miracles. The Competition had sent a pair of their key leaders, Moses and Aaron, to seek permission to get our Rival's people out of Egypt. Pharaoh, an avowed follower of our Enterprising Founder, could have been influenced by the miracles they performed; however, Jannes and Jambres were able to copy many of their miracles, turning staves into serpents, producing frogs, and counterfeiting blood. The point of these miraculous activities is clear. They were doing everything they could to oppose the Competition's agenda, and counterfeiting miraculous deeds turned out to be a stroke of genius. Our agents have successfully employed counterfeiting in almost every era, and it's a marvelous technique for opposition.

Effective resistance often involves turning the tables on the strategy of the opposition, and one of the finest examples of this can be found in the words of one of our Competitor's corporate heroes, a man named Job. You remember, I mentioned him before. He was the object of our Pernicious Founder's special efforts, and our CEO actually succeeded in getting him to wish he had never been born. In fact, the high point of the efforts of the Top Guy Down Below came when this man Job told our Chief Rival, "You have become cruel to me; with the strength of your hand you oppose me."[4] Never mind the obvious falsehood in the man's charges—

we were delighted to see him accuse his CEO of opposition. One of the most effective ways to deflect attention from your own activities is to accuse someone else of the same thing.

Years ago, I worked with a client who managed a small Competition Unit. This man had a particular weakness for what the Competition refers to as "the lust of the flesh." I encouraged him to use his vivid imagination to fantasize himself becoming sexually involved with members of his Competition Unit to whom he was attracted. I also succeeded in convincing him of the importance of devoting much of his sermon time to warning others of the sins of the flesh. He expended a great deal of effort accusing other men of lust and women of wearing provocative clothing and walking seductively. We profited greatly when he finally succumbed to temptation and formed a liaison with one of his parishioners. Naturally, it shocked and disillusioned his congregation. That, Flambeau, is the kind of opposition we like.

You may be interested to know that the black knight our Pernicious Founder is priming for an important future role in our ultimate takeover strategy will make extensive use of the tool of opposition. Their Previous Business Plan describes how he will exalt himself against the Competition's "Prince" and carry out fearful destruction, destroy the mighty of the Competition and their so-called "holy people," magnify himself in his own mind, then make and break a merger contract with the people of the Competition.[5] One of his predecessors, one of our executives named Antiochus, paved the way for this attack by opposing the daily "sacrifices" and rituals of the Competition.[6]

Let me remind you that the ultimate role model for exercising the gift of opposition is our Legendary and Pernicious Founder himself. Zechariah, one of the Competition's executives, described how our Diabolical Leader stood at the right hand of our Chief Rival to oppose one of his top executives, a so-called "high priest" named Joshua.[7] Such cunning, courageous, and blatant opposition demands that we follow in the footsteps of our Enterprising Founder.

Perhaps at this point, Flambeau, you are sold on the value of the gift of opposition but wonder how best to implement it. Let me suggest several principles I've found to be effective.

First, begin cultivating opposition early in the lives of your clients. That's precisely what happened with this young man Timothy. I think it was his father who helped us in this—we certainly received no support whatsoever from his mother or grandmother—but somehow, perhaps through his father's heavy-handed efforts, Timothy learned to respond with opposition. As I indicated earlier, young humans are particularly adept at this. The other day I chuckled when I saw one of my clients trying to convince her two-year-old to go to bed. "I don't want to go to bed," the young one responded. "I'm not sleepy. I want to stay up." When my client suggested, "All right, you can't go to bed, you have to stay up all night," the child reacted by saying, "But I'm tired, I want to go to bed." You see, Flambeau, anything can be opposed.

Second, effective opposition occurs when you keep your clients from thinking before they act. You may recall that our Competition's executive Paul urged his protégé Timothy to correct with humility those who were in opposition so they would repent, know the truth, and escape the snare of our Pernicious Founder.[8] We simply cannot allow that to happen; we must keep them from coming to their senses, changing their minds, and eluding our strategies of influence.

A third effective strategy for utilizing opposition is to urge your clients to say yes but do nothing. You should be familiar with an incident in which our Chief Rival's son faced the opposition of some of our agents and told them about a man who instructed his two sons to work in the vineyard. The first refused, but afterward regretted it and went to work. The second promised to go but never went.[9] From our perspective, the hero of this story was the man who promised to go but never showed up.

I noticed from studying the spreadsheets and personality profiles of your clients at Glencrest that many of them, including Gene, have a natural tendency to promise more than they can deliver. I recall a young woman named René, one of the Competition's most ardent followers, who cleaned houses for a living. She was such a delight to people and seemed so willing to serve. But she had the most irritating and absolutely delightful way of promising people to do things, then conveniently forgetting or just not showing up. She was good at making excuses, and she certainly kept busy enough to be able to present a valid reason. But her opposition caused many of the Competition's followers both annoyance and discouragement.

Some time ago, Christy, one of my clients and an apparently ardent supporter of the Competition, was involved in a meeting with several members of her staff at work, in one of the Competition's advancement organizations. Mark, a man in her department, asked if she could help him gather some data for his quarterly report. She said, "Sure, no problem. I'll have them back to you by the end of the day." Mark left smiling, but Becky, one of her fellow workers asked, "Do you realize what you committed to? Getting those figures together is going to take you at least two hours. With what you told me you already have to do today, there's no way you'll be finished by five. Mark's really going to be disappointed." See how the tactic, which human psychologists identify as passive-aggressive behavior, can work?

A fourth strategy is to demonstrate ambivalence. One of the best ways to do this is simply to say, "I don't know." In this way, your client avoids taking a position, making a commitment, or moving in any direction whatsoever. Teach your client how to win a staring match or a waiting game. For example, when the boss asks them what's going on, or the LCU manager wants to know if they've decided about taking on that class of young people, just have them say, "I don't know," or "I'm not sure." It's amazing how long you can put off activity or commitment that way.

I have one final suggestion for implementing the gift of opposition: Don't ever let them laugh. It's always dangerous to allow things to lighten up. Some time ago, I lost a skirmish when one of my clients attended a counseling session with her LCU manager. She had determined that her husband was hopeless and was prepared to leave him. When the LCU manager asked what irritated her most about her husband, she said, "Jack leaves too many dirty cups and glasses in the sink." When he asked her how often and how many, she simply replied, "Too often and too many."

Things were going fine until he used a little humor. He asked, "You mean he can rack up thirty glasses a day, seven days a week, fifty-two weeks a year? Sounds like a world record holder!" Her resolve cracked; she laughed and said, "No, it's probably just three or four glasses and a cup or two maybe three times a week."

Consider yourself warned, Flambeau, if you're not careful, the warmth of humor can melt the ice of opposition. Incidentally, competition and opposition often go well together. You need to keep that in mind, especially since

Hotspur has done a serviceable job of teaching the tricks of opposition to his clients. You'd better cultivate those specialized defenses, sandbag tactics, negative images, and other opposition techniques so that your clients become more effective in following our Pernicious Leader's example.

>>CONFIDENTIAL MEMO NINE<<

To: flambeau@darkcorp.com
From: scraptus@darkcorp.com
Subject: Winning by Intimidation

Recently our human clients have been utilizing a phrase I'd like to hear more often. It's simple, but it reflects a virtue our Diabolical Founder has both demonstrated and encouraged throughout history. The phrase is "in your face," and it accomplishes what we call intimidation. It's one of the most powerful weapons in your entire arsenal, Flambeau. You must begin using it more frequently to influence Gene and your other clients at the LCU of Glencrest.

Many of our human clients are learning intimidation and making more effective use of it than ever before. Sports figures engage in trash talking, standing over fallen opponents, screaming, and "running up the score"—a delightful practice, I might add. Young gangs of teenagers inflict serious pain on their victims—beating, raping, robbing, shooting, and maiming. These actions certainly are forms of intimidation. In fact, the Current Business Plan of our Competition includes an instance in which a traveler from Jerusalem to Jericho was mugged, robbed, and maimed.[1] One of our early corporate strategies to counter the expansion campaign of our Competitor involved a wide range of intimidation, from throwing their corporate personnel into prison, to forcefully taking their possessions, to actually having some of their key corporate officers put to death.[2]

Surely by now you've been able to pick up the pattern by which we use increasingly strong gifts to turn up the heat against our Competition. The humans who live on the coast understand the difference between a squall, a gale-force wind, and a hurricane. If discouragement doesn't work, try opposition. If that fails, then it's time for intimidation.

To ensure that you have a handle on the concept, let me define it. To intimidate is to prevent a Competitor's objective by using overwhelming force—physical, verbal, emotional, or otherwise—against him.

No one has better exemplified the fine art of intimidation than our CEO Below. Although he began his exemplary career by using manipulation and deceit on Eve, one of the original pair of human clients, he used wave after wave of intimidating circumstances against another of their legendary entrepreneurs, a man named Job. Yes, him again. But there's so much to learn from our work with him. Our Diabolical Founder carefully orchestrated the destruction of Job's property and the deaths of his children, then whispered in the ear of his wife the suggestion that her husband should curse our Chief Rival and die. It was intimidation at its best.

Down through history our Enterprising Founder has always been effective at intimidation, setting the tone for our entire firm, to the extent that the Competition found it necessary to include a special warning about this in their Current Business Plan.[3] Perhaps they thought to insult our CEO Below by describing him as a roaring, prowling lion looking for prey. I can tell you this, Flambeau—he was flattered! In fact, we all were, especially since humans consider the lion to be the king of the jungle. Humans who spend any time in a jungle setting will tell you there's no sound more fearsome. And of course those cats are deadly.

Because the Competition has been so careful to catalog a

great deal of historical information in their Business Plan, they've included a number of people whom we might label "asset strippers," individuals who've used intimidation with dazzling success and become folk heroes in the process—for example, Pharaoh of Egypt, who forced the entire Hebrew division of our Competition into servitude, stripped them of their assets, and then insulted their vice president, Moses. He even questioned the existence of our Chief Rival.[4]

Another man who showed great promise and initiative in the fine art of intimidation was actually a member of our Competition's Israelite division. His name was Korah. With the help of two associates, Dathan and Abiram, he gathered 250 executives and challenged Moses, the CEO over Israel, and Aaron, one of his top administrative aides. Their intimidating showdown pushed our Chief Rival into using force himself.[5]

You may also recall the fine work accomplished by Goliath, a Philistine who brought terror to the hearts of all the men of Israel through his forceful personality, his overwhelming physical presence (he was even taller and stronger than modern professional athletes), and his carefully cultivated use of browbeating verbal attacks.[6] Unfortunately, despite his intimidating skills, he was accidentally killed by an insignificant Israelite representative in a freak accident involving a sling.

One of my favorite intimidators in our Competition's Previous Business Plan was a man named Samson, a heavy-hitting corporate raider from the Israelite division of our Competition, who nonetheless managed to become one of our better corporate assets. You may recall that he once killed a thousand people with the jawbone of a dead donkey. On other occasions he managed to force his way into sexual favors and out of difficult circumstances. Because of his significant intimidation skills, crude though they were, he was able to keep conflict stirred up between the Israelites and the Philistines during most of his lifetime.[7]

You may also recall hearing the name of Absalom in some of your earlier studies. This Israelite executive was particularly skilled at manipulation and deceit, but on occasion he could intimidate with the best of them.

His brother Amnon was also good at inducing fear; in fact, he used it to force his sexual attentions on his half-sister Tamar. After raping her, he insulted her further by kicking her out into the street like a prostitute. This act of intimidation so stirred Absalom that he ordered his brother Amnon assassinated! Later, he threatened his father by blatantly taking King David's concubines in a tent set up for that purpose in a visible location on the palace roof.[8]

Even our Rival's son was forced to deal with intimidation among his inner circle of executives. Two of his leading assistants, James and John, were prepared to call down fire from heaven on one occasion.[9] Another time their executive vice president, Simon Peter, became so irate that he took a sword and attempted to split the head of one of the Temple Enterprise's lower-level functionaries right down the middle! Of course, he missed—he was out of practice—but at least he sliced off the man's right ear.[10]

Now that you've surveyed these excellent historical examples of intimidation, Flambeau, it's important that you understand the foundational traits or qualities that produce this useful force: anger and an absence of conscience.

Peter was furious and out of control when he tried to split open the guy's head because his CEO was about to be arrested. So he didn't bother to listen to all the weak moral teaching he'd been given. Instead, he struck out in a blind rage. Samson never allowed conscience to get in his way, but frequently became enraged when he couldn't have what he felt he was entitled to. Absalom was also a good example of someone who had what human psychologists like to call "sociopathic tendencies," or what we refer to as a properly disabled conscience—an objective we seek to achieve with all our clients.

Flambeau, you may think that our clients today would have difficulty using intimidation. Nothing could be further from the truth. I recall that one client, the vice president of a large distribution firm who also served as a VP in his Competition Unit organization, actually waved a lighted cigar in the faces of fellow board members as he sought to engineer the firing of some LCU management staff members. He finally succeeded in forcing his will on the others. I challenged a group of female clients to use this skill on the young, impressionable wife of a rookie LCU manager who dared enter their Competition Unit wearing makeup. I had three of them surround her as soon as she walked in, and then had the leader tell her, "Go in the bathroom right now and wipe that stuff off your face. We don't allow makeup here." Then I convinced several of the leaders in the same Competition Unit to sit through the service with their faces turned at a ninety-degree angle away from the LCU manager while he spoke. The other attendees got the message, and before long that LCU manager and his wife were history!

On another occasion, I persuaded a rather large matron, a client named Velma, to get "in the face" of the LCU manager's wife. In the process, she actually pushed her back into a pew. I tell you, Flambeau, it took years for that diminutive LCU manager's wife to get over the shock of what she'd been through!

If you haven't seen the opportunities afforded by effective intimidation, Flambeau, you just aren't looking. I can tell you right now, I've been very impressed with Hotspur's successes in implementing an effective, swaggering form of intimidation on the part of his clients. If your clients are to succeed at intimidation, you need to get a handle on some principles that will stand them—and you—in good stead.

First, your clients need to start early. The best time to teach intimidation is during childhood. I'm always delighted when parents slap, pound, drag, yell at, and otherwise abuse their children. Now I'm not talking about the kind of discipline our Competition is talking about in their so-called book of Proverbs. No, I mean the kind that includes generous doses of anger and an absence of conscience, the kind that leaves the parent feeling great and the child ashamed, terrified, and devastated. If we start teaching our children early, then we'll produce teenagers who operate the way Samson did, and who follow the sterling example of the sons of Eli, Hophni and Phinehas, who used personal and sexual intimidation to gain their way with the Israelite division of our Competition.[11]

Second, whenever your clients intimidate, urge them to go all out. They must never pull any punches, show an ounce of compassion, or take any prisoners. They must always inflict maximum damage, never demonstrating the weakness of sympathy or concern for their adversaries.

Third, remind them that there are no limits to the ways in which intimidation can be used. It works effectively in the sexual realm, and it can be used successfully in Competition Unit business or board meetings. It's also a great technique for insisting on their way in the family, and it can even be used on strangers. On a number of occasions I've encouraged some of my clients to put bumper stickers with messages from the Competition on their vehicles, then exercise the skill of intimidation on their roads and highways. Yelling and cutting off traffic, all the while carrying the Competition's banner—it's an absolute delight.

Fourth, remind your clients always to demand what's rightfully theirs. One of our most important values is entitlement, and intimidation can help your clients achieve entitlement in every area of life. Some time ago, when the parents of several of my clients died and the children gathered to distribute the estate, I persuaded the oldest son, Bob, to become increasingly forceful in the discussions with the attorney. Then I prodded his sister Julie to do the same. The result almost rivaled a major human war!

Fifth, remind your clients that whenever they intimidate, the end always justifies the means. After all, if they are convinced that what they think is right or best, they need to be forceful in pushing it through—whether it's a program in the Glencrest Competition Unit or a family decision.

Finally, remind them that intimidation works best when they're willing to show force. I particularly like the incident in which Absalom intimidated his brother with two hundred men.[12] Your client Gene should be an excellent prospect for developing into an effective intimidator. His military background, his forceful personality, his tendency toward anger, and his struggles with conscience leave him ripe for cultivating this fine art.

In closing, let me give you a few contemporary human examples of skilled intimidators. One is Billy the Bully. He's the kind of person who utilizes such tactics as verbally or even physically bombarding and pushing, slamming things, and throwing tantrums.

A second example is Nellie Know-it-all. She and her kind are the "superior" people who believe—and want you to recognize—that they know everything there is to know about anything worth knowing. They are condescending and imposing when they know what they're talking about, and simply pompous if they don't. They have mastered the skill of making those around them feel like idiots.

Then there's Dwight the Difficult. This individual doesn't always have the forcefulness of the hostile, aggressive bully or the assurance of the know-it-all. But he can be effective in setting up roadblocks, dragging his feet, grinding gears, and bringing progress to a halt. He may utilize unrelenting criticism, arguments, or simply complain from the sideline.

Sally the Sniper may actually be one of the most effective of all intimidators; after all, few things are as disconcerting and devastating as a painful attack out of the clear blue from an unknown and unexpected source. The weapon of the sniper is like a rock hidden in a soft snowball—a not-too-subtle dig, a nonplayful tease, a joking insult with enough truth and power to hurt. These things can do lasting damage, yet they're always accompanied by nonverbal messages that say, "This really isn't all that bad." It is a most subtle form of intimidation—but it works.

A final example is Edward the Explosive. He is an individual who, like a volatile chemical, can be set off with little or no cause. His volatility makes him all the more effective as he frequently combines this trait with other intimidation skills.

Incidentally, one of our Diabolical Founder's "golden rules" applies to intimidation. It reads, "Do unto others before they do unto you." In other words, always look for an opportunity to go on the attack.

>>CONFIDENTIAL MEMO TEN<<

To: flambeau@darkcorp.com
From: scraptus@darkcorp.com
Subject: The Gift of Sarcasm

Our clients sometimes have great difficulty learning certain skills, but they must be persuaded to persevere if they are to serve us effectively. Yet occasionally a gift comes along from our Infernal Founder that is just diabolically, delightfully fun, and our clients master it immediately. One of my all-time favorites is the gift of sarcasm.

I doubt whether you have the natural talent for this skill to the degree demonstrated by Hotspur and some of our junior staff, but it's certainly one that you can cultivate and pass on to Gene and his friends.

First, let me suggest a definition for sarcasm. You'll need to pay close attention to the elements. It is pointed humor laced with anger and a carefully camouflaged intent to harm.

The most obvious component in sarcasm is its pointed humor. Like tart cherries in a cherry pie, humor is what gives sarcasm its unique touch. Otherwise, it would simply be called anger. There's nothing wrong with anger, of course, but sarcasm provides our clients with the opportunity to become angry, even vindictive, without appearing that way. It's a lot like the carefully patterned camouflage jackets some of your clients wear when they go hunting or to war.

Since we're clearly at war with our Competition, I've come up with an analogy that I believe demonstrates the way sarcasm works. You may recall from your study of human history how snipers have played an important role in recent wars. They do an excellent job of demoralizing even powerful forces because they hit suddenly and unexpectedly, cause serious but selective harm, then vanish without a trace. That same hit-and-run strategy is precisely what we want to teach our clients.

Now you must understand, Flambeau, that sarcasm, or verbal sniping, isn't designed to replace such effective tools as opposition or intimidation. Rather, it provides an excellent alternative in certain situations.

Sarcasm often works hand in hand with other weapons such as discouragement. For example, you may recall how effectively Thomas, one of our Chief Competitor's vice presidents, combined sarcasm with discouragement. On one occasion, when our Competitors were headed for Jerusalem, they expressed concern over threats to our Arch Rival. Thomas combined sarcasm with discouragement by contributing those immortal words, "Well, let's go up there also, so we may die with him."[1] Unfortunately, most of our Competitors were so dense they totally missed his sarcasm.

Later he provided an even more effective sarcastic barb, one that drew a response from the Chief Rival, who had just announced his plans to leave his management council and return to their corporate headquarters. I tell you, Flambeau, Thomas was absolutely brilliant. He said, "We don't know where you're going; how can we know the way?" I think if you'd been there, you would have seen heads nodding all over the room. It didn't stop our Chief Rival, but at least it planted seeds of doubt in the minds of some of his other vice presidents.[2]

To be candid with you, this is one skill that most people in what the Competition calls biblical days didn't learn to master. In recent days, however, we've made up a lot of lost time. Let me give some examples to show you how it works today.

Some years ago, I had a brilliant physician as a client. He had developed the haughty air that seems to go with the practice of human medicine so much better than their so-called compassion. My client had a young intern working with him who was avidly interested in clinical nutrition. He invested a great deal of time researching the subject and kept bringing articles and studies to my client's attention.

The young man's efforts proved useless, since my client had made up his mind years before that nutritional therapy was practiced only by quacks. For him, real medicine came only in two forms: surgery and drugs. My client put the young upstart in his place during his rounds one day when the young man suggested a nutritional therapy and tried to present the research to substantiate his suggestion.

My client paused, glared at the young man, then, using his voice with dramatic effect, said, "Simpson! Have you been wasting your time hanging out in health food stores again? How will you ever have time to practice medicine? And how many times do I have to tell you this? I don't want to hear any more about this so-called therapeutic nutritional nonsense. Anyone with even basic medical skills can see that the treatment for this patient is straightforward. Next case!"

Of course that was a frontal sniping attack. Sometimes it's more effective when the assault is presented in more subtle fashion. That human poet Pope talked about someone being "damned with faint praise."

I had another client, a verbally skilled female who could use both assault and flattery, often at the same time. After her LCU manager's presentation on Sunday morning, she greeted him at the door with, "Oh, you're just so deep; I can't follow all your teaching—but it certainly makes me feel good!" That remark, especially after a sermon designed to stir up rather than cheer up our Competition, left the poor man shaking his head in bewilderment. On another occasion, in a Competition Unit business meeting while a number of people were speaking at once, she said just loudly enough for the LCU manager's wife to hear, "He has absolutely nothing to say, but he says it so well!"

Flambeau, if your humans leave the object of their sarcasm both hurting and confused, they've probably employed it successfully.

I once had a group of clients in one of our Competitor's advanced management schools (now there's an ideal place for our efforts, Flambeau) who were training to become corporate officers for our Competition. I was able to equip them with the dark skills of sarcasm. Then I set them on one of the more timid executives who taught in the "seminary," as they call it. I figured that because he demonstrated a high degree of what the Competition refers to as humility, he would be an ideal target for their sarcasm. He turned out to be that and more.

During every class session, I would have at least one student (often more) toss out some sarcastic barb such as, "How did you become so much more brilliant than the rest of the faculty?" Or, "What gives you the right to take a position that counters all the apostolic fathers and the current theologians." Or (one of my all-time favorites), "So, how many years did you spend teaching this material in junior high Sunday school class?"

Those little barbs finally began to wear down the professor, and he wound up quitting at the end of the year. That pleased the Head Guy Down Below to no end.

Sometimes, Flambeau, sarcasm merely grazes the intended target. On other occasions, however, it can cause a mortal wound. Your client might not realize that serious damage has been done because the object of the sarcasm may be smiling on the outside while he is bleeding to death on the inside. Incidentally, if you want to develop a real skill in this area, spend some time observing children on the playground at an elementary school. They torment each other unmercifully, and the most vulnerable ones always take the brunt of the sarcasm.

Perhaps you're wondering why we need sarcasm when we have so many other excellent weapons. Let me answer by suggesting three reasons to launch a sarcastic attack. One is anger over circumstances. Let your clients know that few tools are more useful than sarcasm for getting even. They may feel like punching the person in the nose, but a well-chosen barb in the ear can be much more efficient and cost effective.

A second motive for sarcasm is control. Sarcastic barbs provide a superb means for undermining anyone who interferes with your client's objectives. Sometimes just one well-timed verbal shot can eliminate the opposition.

There's a third reason you may want your clients to try sarcasm. Some of them won't care about this one, but many will. Sarcasm is a good way to get attention from those around them. They can bask in the laughter while cultivating the inherent meanness our Enterprising Founder would like to see developed more fully in all the Competition's branches. Carefully chosen words, a biting tone of voice, even funny facial expressions, can attract attention the way honey attracts flies.

Some time ago I had a client whose daughter became interested in two men. One had pledged to serve our Competition; the other was one of my more responsive clients. The latter set out to do whatever it took to make a lot of money. The young woman's mother, who appreciated status and the finer things in life, strongly urged her daughter to marry my client. But the daughter persisted in making plans to marry the other man. At my suggestion, the mother used a nonstop stream of sarcasm to question the young man's ancestry, motivation, love, ability to earn a living, and just about everything else she could think of, plus a few things I suggested to her that she wouldn't have considered.

The result was quite successful, Flambeau. The young lady had been able to resist her mother's frontal assault, but the continual sniping wore her down and actually became a source of irritation between the young suitor who planned to serve our Competition and his intended bride. She broke off the engagement after a particularly vicious quarrel between the two of them over one of the mother's more effective sarcastic barbs.

Flambeau, let me outline some of the desired results of sarcasm. First, it takes away the Competition's joy. If you find that Gene or some of your other clients are beginning to enjoy our Competition's assets, target them with sarcasm. They'll soon become miserable again.

Sarcasm also increases shame. Although the Competition has a brand of shame, the kind we want to manufacture in increasing quantities is the hopeless kind that makes our clients feel helpless and worthless and induces them to give up. And sarcasm is an important ingredient in this process.

And, of course, sarcasm paralyzes. One of its great strengths is that, unlike direct opposition and other frontal assaults, sarcasm can actually freeze the Competition members in their tracks. Sarcasm hardly ever leads to any positive action or response.

Finally, sarcasm seems to enhance human stress, since it's difficult to cope with. Individuals don't seem to know when or from whom the next attack will come, and they wind up expending a great deal of emotional energy worrying about what they heard or what they think they heard. As you can see, Flambeau, sarcasm is an ingenious invention of our Infernal Founder.

Let me suggest ten strategies for employing sarcasm among your clients at Glencrest Competition Unit. First, make them ultra-sensitive to their own pain. Sarcasm is usually generated in response to some irritation or hurt. In fact, in some ways it resembles the pearls that humans prize, which develop because of sand irritating the oysters. Do everything you can to leave your clients as uncomfortable as possible. Let them marinate their minds with past hurts, both real and imagined. Their ruminations will provide fertile ground for the growth of sarcasm.

Second, desensitize your clients to the feelings of others. You must expend every effort to keep them from developing compassion, because it's virtually impossible for compassion and sarcasm to coexist. Rid their minds of any care or concern about how their comments will be taken.

Third, like human snipers, sarcastic individuals must learn to maintain their cover. Teach your clients to use the rituals and social constraints of the Competition Unit. Work and friendship are excellent protected places from which to strike out with their sarcastic barbs. These camouflage techniques include a big smile, a laugh, and comments such as, "I'm just kidding, you know!" Or, "He's really a nice guy. . . ." If you're clever, you'll follow Hotspur's example and cultivate your own collection of original barbs.

A fourth strategy involves teaching your clients the art of

what I like to call third-party sarcasm. Here's how it works. Occasionally your client will be able to pass along a report that resembles gossip but retains the distinctive flavor of the angry, humorous barb. For example, "So-and-so said such-and-such" about another person. In this way, the bullets appear to be flying from several directions at once. The target of the sarcasm becomes confused about what's going on, and the result is devastating. Teach your clients to emotionally demolish other people with comments taken out of context, sharpened to a point, and easily plunged into the heart with an innocent "did you hear what so-and-so said about you?"

Fifth, employ sarcasm in pressure situations for maximum irritation. For example, if your client's husband is exasperated when the car breaks down in rush hour traffic, have her offer a comment such as, "Well, there's nothing like keeping up on maintenance!" Or when a daughter is frantically preparing to go out on a special date, a zinger such as "I'm sure he realizes that every teenager has zits" can really turn up the stress.

Sixth, have your clients cultivate the fine art of the carefully worded put-down. Sarcasm is a great way to let others know who's in—and who isn't. Semi-insulting nicknames can be useful here, as can backhanded compliments such as, "I'm sure you must have gotten a great bargain on that dress!"

Seventh, urge your clients to show no mercy; they must be relentless. A barrage of merciless teasing, put-down humor, and caustic one-liners can penetrate even the strongest emotional armor.

Eighth, show your clients how effective it is to follow sarcasm with more sarcasm. Be sure they don't respond calmly and gently. Help them see the value of the pointed comeback. If all else fails, have them pull out the tried-and-true response: "What? Can't take a joke?"

Ninth, help them understand how to develop a hidden agenda and keep it hidden. They may be holding a grudge, and rightfully so, because of some grievance they've suffered. Sarcasm is an ideal way to keep that grievance from coming to the surface where it might be dealt with. Similarly, sarcasm provides our clients with a marvelous opportunity for exercising control without seeming to be controlling. This way they'll stay in better graces with the Competition Unit while accomplishing our corporate purposes.

Finally, motivate them to sarcastic persistence. Humans have a form of torture called the "death of a thousand cuts." Instead of being killed with a single blow, the victim is forced to endure a thousand small cuts all over his body. He literally oozes to death. The same result can be achieved with sarcasm. Over time, a barb here and a cut there will cause the victim to die slowly. Have your clients keep up the pressure, brandishing the weapon of sarcasm frequently and without a flicker of guilt.

Not to brag, Flambeau, but sarcasm is an innovation that I helped develop and convey to Slerchus and the others who trained your contemporaries (although I've not gotten the credit that I should have for this innovation). Because of the nearsighted policies of the business school, they were never given the opportunity to cultivate this important skill. Back in those days, the Low Command allowed Slerchus and his colleagues to get away with teaching just the basics—intimidation and opposition—thus avoiding the complex subtleties that allow our agents to compete in today's corporate climate.

I've observed that both you and Hotspur have demonstrated

some proficiency at using and teaching sarcasm. Because it's one of our most effective competitive strategies, we need to make sure that your clients employ it well. It comes a little too easily for Hotspur. I've no doubt our golden boy will be offering lessons to the rest of us before long.

>>CONFIDENTIAL MEMO ELEVEN<<

To: flambeau@darkcorp.com
From: scraptus@darkcorp.com
Subject: The Gift of Stonewalling

One of our most undervalued assets is stonewalling. I'm convinced of its superiority for undermining the effectiveness of our LCUs. Sure, we all recognize the importance of intimidation, gossip, controlling, discouragement, and even sarcasm. But sometimes the best thing for our clients to say is nothing at all.

I suspect that you haven't even considered using the gift of stonewalling with Gene or any of your other clients at Glencrest. Let me urge you to add it to your arsenal immediately. I've just received a memo from Hotspur detailing how well it has worked with his number-two client. I give him high marks for seeing its value.

Hotspur's clients are part of a Competition Unit where an enthusiastic young woman was appointed to their educational committee. She carefully researched her subject, then made a presentation to the Competition Unit board that could have revolutionized their educational efforts. She wanted to remove a lot of the archaic methods we've been keeping in place for years and replace them with much more effective, modern methods. After Alice had finished her presentation, she asked the board for comments or questions.

Because I was sitting in a supervisory capacity, I would have expected Hotspur to have one of the men use intimidation, another discouragement, and still another control. Instead, he had them all clam up. They showed no enthusiasm, offered no argument, and made no positive or negative statements. Flambeau, I wish you could have seen the look on her face!

One board member kept looking at his watch, another stared out the window, one just looked at her, and one shuffled his notes on the table. As the silence stretched on, Alice's confidence and enthusiasm drained away like water from a sink. The ultimate result was that she gave up her efforts to reform the educational and youth programs, and the status quo, which favors us over the Competition, was maintained.

I think the clam, that primitive little bivalve creature, provides an excellent role model for our human clients. Whenever clams encounter any kind of probe, foreign body, or disagreeable situation, they close down. Or as humans like to put it, they "clam up." It's one of the most disruptive tactics possible, and Hotspur and his clients have used it with dazzling success.

The best thing about stonewalling, or clamming up, is that our clients can use it without a twinge of moral guilt, and it carries no negative image the way intimidation and gossip do. In fact, Flambeau, your clients can exercise the gift of stonewalling and appear to be as committed to the Competition as anyone. In effect, their silence raises a wall of stone directly in the path the Competition seeks to move his humans along. Granted, it's a defensive rather than an offensive strategy, but it provides a key component in our campaign of harassment against the Competition.

Sometimes stonewallers say nothing. On other occasions, they may respond with a "yep," a "nope," or perhaps a grunt. Best of all, Flambeau, they don't have to be shy, quiet, or introverted. Almost anyone can engage in stonewalling. Those who are used to employing their tongues may require some mental reprogramming, but it can be done.

Our Competition's Business Plan doesn't contain a lot of examples of stonewalling. My suspicion is that Timothy, the young protégé of their Chief Vice President, Paul, had a tendency to use this technique because he seemed to need frequent "stirring up."[1] I think there were some people in one of the original franchises Paul founded (Thessalonica) who had mastered this passive strategy and combined it with gossip and some of our other tools.[2]

On one occasion, when our forces engineered the arrest of Paul, he was presented before one of our officers, a man named Agrippa, for a hearing. After listening to Paul, Agrippa combined stonewalling with sarcasm, using words the Competition has quoted often: "You almost persuade me to become a Christian."[3] After making this statement, Agrippa and the others who were with him didn't linger to listen to the appeals of our Competition's spokesman. Instead they left the hearing without comment.

Let me suggest several reasons for using this technique, Flambeau. One is that your clients can avoid being hurt or confronted with painful insights. Ted, a client of mine, had used the company postage meter to mail all of his personal Christmas gifts. When the boss confronted him, I reminded him that he certainly couldn't admit it, or the boss would yell at him. If he lied about it, he'd feel guilty. So I whispered into his mind that if he said nothing at all, the boss would probably talk for a while, perhaps lecture him, but eventually give up and go away. That's exactly what happened.

Another benefit is that clamming up provides an excellent tool for inspiring aggression. There's nothing quite as delightful as watching frustration and irritation grow in the face of your client's stony-faced silence. It's one of life's great pleasures.

And stonewalling is a superb tool for control. After all, if you're saying nothing, you're really taking charge. Your clients need to see how effectively stonewalling and control can be used in tandem.

Finally, stonewalling helps your clients avoid looking at themselves and the truth. Whenever they verbalize their secret desires or fears, they run the risk of actually owning them. It's far safer to maintain silence.

While mastering the fine art of stonewalling, Flambeau, your clients will also need to learn how to use nonverbal communication. There are two basic kinds: gestures and facial expressions. Gestures range from the shaken fist, the down-turned palm, the drumming fingers, or the shrug—with or without hands raised. Simply looking at a watch can be devastating.

Facial expressions include a wrinkled brow, a down-turned mouth, a horizontally shaken head, with the shake ranging from subtle to vigorous, even a flushed face. These gestures can convey a wide range of messages, from "I could care less" to "I'm furious," and from "I'm thinking" to "I'm stalling for time."

The best thing about nonverbal clues is that they contribute to the overall stonewalling effect. Seldom are those to whom your client is listening able to figure out what's going on in your client's mind. Best of all, if they guess wrong, they wind up creating problems that didn't even exist. Imagine what happens if the object of your client's stonewalling treats him as though he was angry when in fact he is simply timid. That's like pouring gasoline on a fire!

Some time ago, Ron, one of my clients, was called in for his annual performance review by his boss, a consultant for the Competition. After he assessed Ron's year, he wanted to get Ron's viewpoint. Did he agree with the assessment? Did he have any ideas for improving his performance?

I had prepared Ron in advance for this point, and I reminded him to shift his mind into neutral and keep it there. He sat staring at a picture on the wall and drumming his fingers on the table in front of him. His boss couldn't help wondering, Is he angry? Is he trying to control me? Is he afraid of losing his job?

Every time Ron felt moved to speak, I reminded him to clam up. When his boss tried open-ended questions, I had him maintain silence. When the boss attempted a lengthy pause, allowing the silence to grow while he stared at Ron, I had Ron simply stare back with a bland look on his face. On a couple of occasions, I had him seem like he was about to talk, then stop. The boss looked as though he were about to explode! Finally, when the boss persisted, I allowed Ron to give the most effective verbal response a stonewaller can use. When the boss said, "Ron, what are you thinking?" I had him say, "I don't know."

"What's on your mind right now?"

"I don't know."

"How do you react to what I've just said?"

"I really don't know."

Finally the boss gave up in disgust, signed off on the review, handed Ron a copy, and ended the interview.

By the way, Flambeau, stonewalling can operate in the relational arena almost as effectively as it works conversationally. Some time ago, I had a client who was employed by a publishing company affiliated with our Competition. They were to make a presentation to a media organization that could help them greatly expand their influence. Theresa, my client, never turned down a request; so when her boss, James, sought to enlist her assistance, she agreed. Theresa promised to pull all the research together, develop a presentation for James, produce handouts and transparencies, and provide all the resources James needed to make the presentation.

About a week before the presentation was to be given, James dropped by Theresa's office and asked, "How's it going?"

"Just fine," Theresa replied.

"You have all the details from accounting?"

"Well, I think so. I'm going to get back with someone from accounting this afternoon or tomorrow."

On the big day, James was set to make the presentation. He was somewhat apprehensive but pleased when he heard that the CEO planned to go along. He was glad that Theresa had offered her help. What he didn't suspect was that I had influenced Theresa's strategies.

Ten minutes before they were due in the boardroom to make the presentation, James became anxious. Five minutes later, he began to wonder if perhaps he had told Theresa they'd meet at her office instead of his.

When he walked down to her office, he found her hunched over her computer, typing away. "What are you doing?" he asked. "Weren't we supposed to meet five minutes ago? Surely you're not having to make last-minute changes?"

"Oh, hi, James. I'm sorry," Theresa replied, "I lost track of the time. No last-minute changes, I'm just working on something for Bob in human resources. They're short a person today, and he asked if I could help him out. He needs this real soon. Can you wait just a minute?"

"Bob in human resources? A few minutes? Theresa, we've got to leave now or we'll be late. Where's the proposal?"

Theresa began digging through the papers that covered

her desk, shuffling through things. "Oh, here's one. Here's another." She pulled several pieces of paper together. Some were quite wrinkled.

You should have see the look on James's face, Flambeau! "This is a rough draft! Look at these mistakes! And where are the transparencies?"

"I'm sorry, James. I didn't get a chance to do them. Secretarial services is going through a reorganization. I didn't have the heart to ask them."

It was a delightful disaster, Flambeau, and the lessons are obvious. You can have your clients stonewall by getting them to promise the moon, then fail to deliver. Sometimes that can be just as effective as saying nothing. Then they can clam up when they're confronted with their passive response. Result? The Competition is frustrated; we succeed.

>>CONFIDENTIAL MEMO TWELVE<<

To: flambeau@darkcorp.com
From: scraptus@darkcorp.com
Subject: The Gift of Flirtation

The next tool to consider in our ongoing struggle to overtake the Local Competition Unit is radically different from stonewalling. In some ways it resembles sarcasm, gossip, or gab. I'm talking about the gift of flirtation, a useful tool invented by Our Infernal Founder in response to the Chief Competition's first strategic mistake—from our point of view at least—of creating our clients "male and female." Since he designed them with sexuality, our Enterprising Chairman saw the opportunity to utilize this intense human drive, one we don't have, as part of our corporate infrastructure. It's become one of our greatest assets, and it frequently leads to personal confusion and what the Competition refers to as "moral failures."

Our Competitors have included a great deal about this matter of sexuality in their Business Plan. You know it must be quite effective because they devote so much space to discussing it and warning against it in various ways.

One of the first examples of the value of flirtation and its industrial-strength version, seduction, can be found in their PBP. Judah, a man who became one of our Competition's most prominent agents, fell prey to the seductive wiles of his daughter-in-law Tamar, who took off her widow's veil, disguised herself as a prostitute, and manipulated him into a sexual liaison.[1]

Sometime later in the corporate history of our Competitors,

another woman named Tamar fell prey to a combination of attempted flirtation and intimidation that ultimately led to her brother raping her, then shaming and hating her, actions that furthered our cause and hindered the Competition.[2]

Solomon, one of our shrewdest Competitors, had a great deal to say about the flirtatious woman. He pointed out the power of her verbal frivolity, acknowledged her lack of commitment, and pointed out how her actions further our corporate objectives.[3] Later, he described her conversation as "dripping honey" and "smoother than oil," graphic word pictures of how effectively she can turn people to our Chairman's objectives.[4] Flambeau, I must agree with Solomon's assessment that her ways are unstable and deceptive to those who are so attracted by them.[5] That's why they can be such powerful tools to influence Gene and your other clients at the LCU at Glencrest.

There aren't very many better ways of entrapping those who are leaning toward our corporate agenda than flirtation, especially a flirtation that leads to seduction and ends up in what the Competition calls an immoral relationship.[6]

One of our Competitor's vice presidents, Solomon, recognized that flirtation has three essential elements. The first is a flattering tongue; the second, alluring beauty; and the third, physical gesture.[7] Solomon must have written from experience when he spoke of these very commendable and useful gifts. Certainly our contemporary agents have done a great deal to cultivate the exercise of all of these elements in modern society. Young, impressionable women (and men) learn early the gestures of flirtation; the value of sensual physical contact; the absolute importance of attractive physical appearance accompanied by seductive dress; and the appropriate use of innuendoes, flattery, and allurement.

Motion pictures, novels, and other forms of literature have lifted flirtation to an art form, and I'm pleased to report that our clients usually don't require a great deal of additional work to become proficient in this area.

I've found the use of two examples from the Enemy's Business Plan to be very effective. One is the so-called "immoral woman," or seductress, whose crafty heart, revealing attire, and words of blatant seduction cause the object of her attention to be drawn to her physical and verbal attractions until she has seduced him.[8] The other model for flirtatious behavior is found in our Opposition's Current Business Plan in the words of their vice president, Paul. He wrote to his protégé Timothy about those who love pleasure more than the Competition and who have learned, as he put it, "to creep into households and make captives of gullible women loaded down with sins, led away by various lusts. . . ."[9]

Several of my clients, both male and female, have demonstrated great proficiently in this kind of flirtation. One was a LCU manager (there have been many of these, as you might suspect) who effectively utilized his people skills to gain the confidence of some of the younger women in his Competition Unit. He began by complimenting them on their appearance and diligence, then he invited them to share their deepest emotional concerns and needs with him, all with the motive of escalating the sensual component of their relationship to a higher level. Before long he had succeeded in physically seducing a number of them, thereby undermining their allegiance to the Competition. He found that this conquest gave him an aura of power, and he used his sensual and flirtatious skills to become one of our most effective agents. It took years for the Competition's internal security to catch up with him.

Another of my clients, whom I'll call Bobby, never became physically involved with women, but he specialized in double entendre, risqué jokes, and suggestive physical compliments. As an added asset, his own physical attractiveness caused women to become interested in him. Our Competitor quickly introduced guilt into their lives to let them know they were doing wrong, but the scale and the scope of the man's seductive power made him almost irresistible.

Another woman, the secretary to an important executive in the Competition's publishing ventures, presented herself as a person of integrity and innocence. However, her skill at seductive physical contact, her flirtatious language, and her boastful statements to third parties about her relationship with her boss ultimately caused him to resign from his job because of a perceived scandal. To be candid, Flambeau, she didn't require much assistance from us, and her lack of discretion played right into our hands.

There is an effective tool that can be used in concert with flirtation: anger. I recall a former client, a female therapist named Monica, who, to use the terminology of our clients, frequently "came on" to her own counseling clients, her husband's male friends, and men in her Competition Unit. Her body language, vocabulary, and appearance communicated a resounding "I'm available." Her strategy was to lead men on to a certain point, then verbally and physically lower the boom on them. She had been victimized sexually by her father as a child, and I was able to capitalize on her resentment toward him to help her refine these tactics.

You see, Flambeau, there are a number of flirtatious techniques that can be used effectively by either sex—and please disabuse yourself of that quite antiquated notion that flirtation is a female-only sport. Men are just as adept, which leads to deliciously destructive results. The most effective technique for men to use against women is touch. This technique is so effective that Paul, the Competition's vice president, warned against men touching women.[10] Part of your responsibility, Flambeau, is to ensure that when your male clients engage in physical contact with women in their Competition Unit or elsewhere, their minds revert to their most basic drives, so that they seek to fulfill their own desires rather than communicate compassion. You should also urge them to look for opportunities to move beyond the bounds of propriety and see how far they can take things.

Usually the most effective way for a woman to flirt with a man is through her appearance. Our Chief Competitor warned against men looking on a woman with lust.[11] If we are to believe our Chief Competitor—and, according to Our CEO Below, there are times when we should take his words at face value—we do well to urge our female clients to take every step to present themselves physically in such a way as to cause the males around them to consider and even visualize the sexual possibilities between them. After all, if we succeed in motivating the women to tantalize men to the point the Competition defines as lust, we've won the battle. My experience indicates that if flirtation is present, lust isn't far behind.

As I mentioned earlier, flattery and deceit can play an important role in effective flirtation, as can the subtle gestures our clients refer to as "body language." In fact, it would be in your best interests to do everything in your power to urge your female clients to avoid modesty at all costs. Help them to see it for the archaic, inhibiting throwback it is—of absolutely no use in modern times. In this regard, I've always found it helpful to attach the words "Puritan" and "Victorian" to the term "modesty." Today's humans don't have a clue what the words "Puritan" and "Victorian" actually meant in their historical context, but we've succeeded, primarily through our entertainment operatives, in creating the impression that anything connected to them is obviously laughable and passé.

I almost forgot to alert you to one of the greatest, most effective uses of flirtation. Be sure to encourage your male and female clients who are of mature age and who have influence over young individuals—teenagers and younger—to use flirtation and seduction toward them. Although some of the mature clients will not be susceptible to this technique because of the influence of the value system of the Enemy, quite a few of them will be.

Case in point: Harlan was a respected husband, father, Competition Unit member, board member, and middle-level executive for a large corporation. First, I tried encouraging him to flirt with people his own age. When he failed to respond, I realized that his activities with the Competition Unit youth group and junior Sunday school placed him in an influential position with younger individuals who were more gullible. Not only did his flirtatious activities distract them from responding to the Competition but also he actually wound up becoming physically involved with two of the teenagers and one of the subteens. I cannot begin to describe the stir his activities created among the Competition Unit! Does Harlan's profound capitulation surprise you, Flambeau? You have no idea how strong our influence can be.

This brings me to the subject of the benefits of flirtation. Although they should be obvious to you, Flambeau, I'd like to spell them out.

First, as in the case of Harlan, flirtation on the part of

married people is actually a form of breaking the marriage vow, which the Competition makes humans take, promising to "forsake all others." Even if they don't become sexually involved, they still have engaged in the pursuit of someone to whom they aren't married.

In the case of unmarried people, flirtation causes their thoughts to become centered on the sensual rather than on the spiritual. This result is particularly valuable for clients who are young and at the point of considering a lifelong commitment to the Competition. In many instances, our agents (such as Hotspur) have demonstrated an uncanny ability to exploit the sensual to undermine the spiritual. I'm expecting you to do likewise.

This shift in focus from spiritual to sensual also works with married individuals. Flirtation can cause many of them to become far more outwardly focused, fitting in with the plans of our Top Guy Below rather than opening up to the Competition's feeble attempts to develop their internal characters. I suggest that you study the writings of Peter, one of the Competition's early vice presidents. Notice his insistence on chaste conduct and his cautions against outward appearance, jewelry, and clothing.[12] Then turn those words around and seek to instill the opposite traits in your clients. I'm sure that you—and we—will be pleased with the results.

Another thing, Flambeau: remember that flirtation helps prepare your clients for deeper involvement in the sensual realm. Our Enterprising Founder has always been able to exploit the sexual susceptibility of the Competition's clients. You may recall that he used it effectively with one of our Competitor's top people, the Israelite king named David. He's using it just as effectively today.

Finally, flirtation capitalizes on the vulnerabilities of our clients. Because of their family circumstances as children, many of them are starved for love and attention. This condition causes them to be attracted to flirtation and seduction like moths to a light or ants to a picnic.

One more thing, Flambeau. Remember one of the most basic principles established in the beginning by our Debased CEO: Everything designed by the Competition has to be twisted before it's of any use to us. In most cases a slight twist or distortion is better than an outright attack against the Competition's directives. I'm inclined to think that those who trained Hotspur and some of the other recent graduates of our business school failed to pay attention to this principle. Old Slerchus and his bunch were content to use aggressive, hot-and-heavy seduction techniques. Oh, they've had their successes, but not with the Competition's committed followers. It's much more common for humans to stand up to obvious, crass assaults on their standards. Prostitution, for example, isn't much use here, although it's been valuable in other sectors outside the Competition's sphere.

These dinosaur demons don't seem to understand the contemporary application of the old idea. Emotional affairs, which opposition employees can rationalize as a way to meet their "needs" without violating Competition directives, frequently lead our clients into sexual involvement. Of course, flirtation is a key way to kindle this process. It's like striking a match near gasoline. No need to let them see the can of gas—just let some fumes waft their way. They won't sense the danger at all, but the fumes are more explosive than the liquid itself.

So don't neglect flirtation, Flambeau. Make it a priority item in your arsenal of client abilities. I don't think even you can imagine the devastation it brings.

>>CONFIDENTIAL MEMO THIRTEEN<<

To: flambeau@darkcorp.com
From: scraptus@darkcorp.com
Subject: Lying, the Foundational Gift

I intend to wrap up my communiqués by underscoring our fundamental corporate value: lying. Nothing plays a more vital role in our corporate strategy. In a sense, lying provides the foundation for all of the other strategies and abilities we've been discussing. Every successful takeover campaign, every element of our strategic diversification, and every carefully orchestrated advance against the Competition has been fueled by this important value. That's why I've saved it for last.

Perhaps you wonder, Flambeau, why lying is so important. The first and most important answer is that it best represents the character of Our Enterprising Founder. Perhaps you recall the incident in which our Chief Competition labeled the Boss a liar and "the father of it."[1] Although the Competition likes to spread their so-called "truth-based message," our competing strategies are always best served by using deceit on a scale and scope beyond the imagination of the enemy. I think it's safe to say that nothing will have a greater influence on your clients at Glencrest, including Gene, than the proper use of deceit.

As I mentioned, the Top Guy Down Below has always furthered his agenda through deceit. It was his initial tool (and an effective one) with the first humans. As you recall from studying our corporate history, our Chairman disguised himself as a beautiful creature, a snake to be exact, to worm his way into the confidence of the first woman. In cunning fashion, he forced her to question the Competition's mandate forbidding her to eat from the tree that could give her a firsthand knowledge of our corporate policy.[2] When she replied that the Competition had forbidden her to eat of it or even touch it under penalty of death, he replied suavely and confidently, "You will not surely die." Cleverly mixing a measure of fact with this blatant prevarication, he warned the client that the Competition actually wanted to keep her from knowing good and evil, insinuating that it was a marvelous ability that he himself possessed. Since that first successful use of out-and-out deceit, our Chairman has insisted that all our strategies be based on lying.

There's another reason why lying is important for our corporate agenda, Flambeau. It's probably the element of our strategy that the Competition most hates. After all, they fly their corporate flag as the so-called "banner of truth." Earlier I mentioned Solomon, one of their most prominent vice presidents and a significant contributor to their Previous Business Plan. When he listed seven things their CEO hates, lying was second on the list![3] Only pride, another of our Head Honcho's top values, finished higher on the Competition's hate list. In case you need to be reminded, pride and deceit can be used as an effective one-two punch against our clients' defenses. It's always good to exercise more than one ability to achieve our agenda. Remember Solomon's axiom that lying lips are an abomination to the Competition.[4]

Solomon's predecessor, David, almost seemed to have a fixation on deceit, expressing his own hatred of lying[5] while asking the Competition to remove it from his personal strategies.[6] Flambeau, you must at all costs avoid allowing Gene or any of your clients to come to such a point.

Another value of lying is that few things have done more harm in the history of our human clients. The Competition included an extensive section in their corporate bylaws requiring restitution, repentance, and all sorts of other compensatory activities whenever any of their corporate people were caught exercising deceit.[7] The Competition's Business Plan chronicles several instances that illustrate the positive benefits of deceit. In one incident, an agent for the Competition was motivated to violate his vows by an experienced double agent of ours, who'd been engaged in a clandestine operation. [8]

In another instance, the Competition allowed us to use four hundred of their agents to deceive Kings Ahab of Israel and Jehoshaphat of Judah to go into battle together at a place called Ramoth-Gilead, a battle that ultimately cost Israel a major defeat and King Ahab his life.[9]

Later in their corporate history, our Chief Competitor accused his first business group, Israel, of engaging in numerous tactics that allied them with us rather than with him, including blatant and chronic lying.[10] The value of lying, for our own corporate culture, can be seen in the fact that one of the Competition's vice presidents, Paul, urged his clients in Ephesus to put away lying and speak truth.[11] Clearly therefore, our agenda must include urging our clients to forget about telling the truth and to speak lies.

Not only has deceit played an important role in our corporate past, but it provides the foundation for our Chairman's plan for the future. When Our Head Honcho unveils the final stage of his business plan, he will build much of the strategy around his ultimate protégé, who will include power, signs, lying wonders, and unrighteous deception in his arsenal.[12]

I was amazed when I counted all of the warnings our Chief Competitor gave his followers against dishonesty. Job, who was the object of our Infernal Founder's personal attention, promised to avoid speaking deceitfully[13] while accusing his friends of choosing the tongue of the crafty.[14] And notorious David, the vice president who played such a prominent role in our Competitor's plans, warned his followers to keep their lips from speaking deceit.[15] One of David's contemporaries lamented how his associates flattered him with their mouths and lied to him with their tongues.[16] As we noted, David's son Solomon explained that the Enemy hates a lying tongue.[17]

One of the Competition's most effective agents, Jeremiah, observed our success with him and other enemy agents during an earlier era. We were delighted with his lament that "everyone will deceive his neighbor and will not speak the truth. They have taught their tongue to speak lies; they weary themselves to commit iniquity."[18] We certainly had things going our way in those days, Flambeau, and the key was getting our clients to practice deceit. As one forecaster explained, "One speaks peaceably to his neighbor with his mouth, but in his heart he lies in wait."[19] That's what we must cultivate in this current generation of clients. We want them to learn to use their tongues like the arrows of an earlier time or the bullets of today, spreading pain and confusion all around.

Apparently we are succeeding here on this continent where our major responsibility lies. Perhaps you've heard of the research conducted by two humans who wrote a book humorously titled *The Day America Told the Truth*. To be honest, Flambeau, we weren't too happy when that book was published because it unveiled the widespread penetration of our strategy of dishonesty. You'd be amazed at how many people, including dedicated followers of our Competition, don't mind stretching the truth or telling an outright lie to further their own agenda—which, of course, furthers ours.

Even their so-called ministers are not exempt; in fact, some of them make the best liars, and not just in their pulpits. Some time ago, I was assigned to one of the Competition's agents with the express purpose of preventing his son, who seemed to have many of the same abilities as his father, from following in his father's footsteps. I used a simple tactic: Encourage the father to keep promising to take his son fishing or to a ball game and then convince him, when the time came to keep his promise, that he was too busy. It was so easy. I simply saw to it that there was always an urgent phone call, an important Competition Unit task to care for, or some other disruption—but still I pointed out to this LCU manager that the best thing for his son (and his own esteem) was to keep promising he'd spend time with him—soon. Of course, he never did. Before long the son caught on and became embittered toward both his dad and our Chief Competitor, whom he saw his father representing.

Perhaps one of its most important advantages is that lying produces pain. Ultimately, it hurts both the liar and the one lied to. For example, the husband who is having an affair may lie to his wife about his schedule and financial expenditures. She is harmed because the marriage relationship is built on a foundation that will crumble whenever the truth is exposed; he is hurt because he is allowed to persist in a course of action that will ultimately fail.

One of the greatest lies in human history was the one that our agent, Adolph Hitler, told British Prime Minister Neville Chamberlain in order to conceal his plans to attack Czechoslovakia. Hitler met with Chamberlain and gave his word that peace could be preserved if the Czechs agreed not to mobilize their troops. Chamberlain later told his people that, in his estimation, Hitler was a man who could be trusted, a man who meant what he said. Because our CEO himself had groomed Hitler in the skill of deceit, his lie opened the door to a massive world war that furthered our corporate agenda beyond our wildest hopes and for a time brought the Competition's plans to a virtual standstill.

Flambeau, you must convince your clients that lying not only is an acceptable strategy but also can and should be used in a variety of arenas. Convince your clients who are parents, for example, that they need not burden their children with the truth concerning family activities or finances. Urge physicians to avoid telling their patients the actual state of their medical condition. Be sure your teenage clients know the value of concealing the true nature of their activities and associates from their parents. See to it that Gene—and, for that matter, each of your other clients—knows how appropriate it is to lie to his LCU manager about such things as why he failed to attend Competition Unit the previous week, or why he can't become involved in teaching a class or working with the youth.

One of my major concerns, Flambeau, is that your clients not only lie but also learn to lie effectively. Just concealing information or falsifying facts, the two most common ways of lying, are not enough. Your clients must have their eyes trained on bigger and better things. They must learn to lie with a certain panache. After all, they reflect on you and your corporate standing.

Let me offer some suggestions for you to pass along to your clients that will help them lie with more confidence. First, they should avoid the so-called values espoused by the Competition. One reason Hitler was so effective at lying is that he did not share the social, ethical, or spiritual values of his contemporaries. Because his agenda, like that of our

Infernal Father, was limited to personal gain, he was able to lie better than most other people.

Another important principle is that those who lie should avoid having to conceal some strong emotion. For example, I once had a client named Priscilla who used a series of lies to cover up her affair with her husband's best friend. Since her primary motivation was anger toward her husband because of an affair he had covered up for years, and because she also felt intense guilt—something we need to train our clients not to feel—she wound up betraying herself. Flambeau, most lies fail because of some emotional leak. The stronger the emotion or the greater the number of different emotions, the more likely that the lie will be uncovered.

A third consideration: Be sure that your clients are careful to avoid compounding lies. It's extremely difficult to remember the exact details of a lie, so they should keep things simple. The complex lie or the lie told to cover up another lie can lead to confusion and exposure of the truth. I recall a colleague's client, a policeman, who was called to testify against several officials charged with criminal behavior. He admitted to two instances of criminal behavior himself, taking a bribe and extorting money. He stuck to his story while cooperating with federal prosecutors to bring several organized criminals to trial. Later, however, investigators proved not only that he had committed many more crimes, but also that the federal prosecutors had cooperated in covering his criminal behavior to use his testimony against a man who actually was innocent. Of course, by then it was too late. We were very pleased with what we had accomplished. Only by keeping his story simple were we able to utilize his lying effectively. He didn't go into a lot of detail but just kept insisting that he had only committed the two activities. It worked well.

Here are some additional tips for strengthening your clients' lying skills so they will be better able to further our corporate aims.

First, keep them from spending any time considering our Competition's corporate Business Plan. Because our Chief Competitor himself labeled their Plan as "truth,"[20] and because their vice president David seemed to view their corporate bylaws as a tool for removing the human tendency to lie, we must stifle any efforts to use this resource. [21]

Second, a sincere look and tone of voice can often effectively mask lying. Have your clients smile, give a firm handshake, and sound sincere. After all, eye contact and body language can go a long way toward covering up a lie.

Third, we found that the use of phrases such as "I'm telling you the truth" or "Let me be very honest with you," although often indicating falsehood, tend further to convince the individual lied to that what they are hearing is true. School your clients in the appropriate, frequent use of such phrases.

Fourth, sometimes you can have your clients lie effectively by telling the truth but with a twist. For example, Ginny was suspicious over the phone calls her husband, Brad, kept receiving. When she asked him who was calling, he said sarcastically, "I'm just talking to my girlfriend; she calls me all the time." Although in one sense he was telling the truth, he was able to use sarcasm to protect his deceit.

Closely related to these techniques are half-truths and incorrect inferences. Here's one you can use: I once had a client whose mother painted—horribly, I might add. The mother pointedly asked her daughter, "What do you think of my pictures?" The daughter simply grasped her mother's arm and emoted deeply, "Mother, Mother, Mother." Although she left her mother with the impression that she was deeply and emotionally moved, actually all she was doing was covering her contempt for her mother's artistic efforts. Some people don't consider this to be lying; however, our corporate policy is to chalk it up to our side because these efforts do involve a deliberate attempt to mislead.

But a word of warning. It is absolutely vital for your clients to keep their stories straight when they lie. I had one client who caused me no end of embarrassment when he told three different Competition staff members three different accounts of why he and his wife had missed worship services in previous weeks. After all, it would be a stretch when they compared notes to believe that extended illness, vacation, and a sick parent all happened at the same time. I've found it helpful to urge the most unsteady liars among my clients to memorize lines as if they were part of a play. After all, in one sense, they are engaged in acting!

Which reminds me. Teach your clients to guard the expressions on their faces. You may recall the legend about the puppet named Pinocchio, whose nose supposedly grew as he lied. Actually, telling falsehoods offers no proven physical sign—no facial expression, gesture, or muscle twitch that, taken by itself, conclusively proves an individual is lying. Still, skilled liars must be careful to guard the look on their faces. After all, the face is the primary site for the display of human emotion. Faces and voices typically tell listeners how speakers feel about what they are saying. To a lesser extent, a tense body and a strained voice can give the game away. However, our studies indicate that words and facial expressions are more likely to betray your client than anything else. That's where firm control needs to be exercised.

Those who want to lie effectively must also be careful to avoid the detestable "Freudian slip," that inadvertent statement prompted by the subconscious. As you know, it's named after one of this past century's most formidable theorists who succeeded in focusing attention on the self and its more refined drives—always a good development for us. His theory was that many individuals who are trying to conceal a lie wind up giving it away through seemingly inadvertent but subconsciously purposeful slips of the tongue. As you know, we've come a long way in erasing any fixed line between right and wrong in human thinking, which should help in this regard since the self—its wants, needs, desires—will become the only source of truth. I always love to hear a client glibly repeat that wonderful mantra, "What's true for me may not be true for you, and vice versa." How splendidly stupid! At the admirable rate we're going, the "Freudian slip" will soon be a thing of the past.

Other ways by which skilled liars often give away their prevarication include tirades in which the deceiver gets carried away by his emotions, and convoluted answers or more sophisticated evasions whereby the individual attempts to use intellectual skills to dazzle the listener. Sometimes even a pause at the wrong place can be a tip-off. Other factors that can give away a lie include slight gestures such as a yes-nod or a no-headshake when saying the opposite of the physical gestures. Keep working with your clients to ensure that they avoid these common hazards.

Another dead giveaway to lying is blushing. The Competition identifies blushing as a sign of personal shame.[22] And sometimes even our most skilled deceivers have been detected when a blush has given them away.

Finally, as with everything, practice makes perfect. Your

charges at LCU have demonstrated flashes of talent, even brilliance, when it comes to the art of lying. Yet, unlike Hotspur and others of your contemporaries, you have shown little tendency to encourage these abilities. Despite the deficiencies inherent in his training under Slerchus and company, Hotspur has become almost satanic in his ability to deceive. I, of course, have the experience and ability to spot his deceptions. But he is good at it, probably because he has done it so often.

Practice is the key, Flambeau. Practice, practice, and more practice. Skilled liars must take great care to develop and memorize their false story lines. I've found that most liars don't anticipate all the questions they may be asked or the unexpected incidents with which they must deal. A gifted liar must have prepared and rehearsed responses for more contingencies than he will likely encounter. It's dangerous for your clients to be inventing answers on the spot. Frequently, their responses will be inconsistent with what they have said in the past and clues will slip out that will reveal their fraud.

I know that Gene is capable of skilled deception, Flambeau. This certainly is one area in which I expect nothing less than magnificent success on your part, not that you've had any such thing up to this point.

I would be less than honest not to pass on to you the suggestion by some down the chain of demand that Hotspur be given your assignment. He's ambitious, Flambeau; I don't have to remind you of that. Just like every other young demon who idolizes our Top Guy Below, he'd like to move down further. Takeovers are, of course, a fact of life in our profession, but you need not worry about my regard for you. Your position is quite secure. Although our colleagues may thrive on plotting against their associates, I wouldn't dream of losing the close working relationship we've developed. We've great things ahead of us—if you're half the brainy demon I take you to be. You can count on me.

>> RETURNED MAIL <<

To: flambeau@darkcorp.com
From: mailsort@darkcorp.com
Subject: Unknown address

The address <scraptus@darkcorp.com> is not a current address.

>>CONFIDENTIAL MEMO<<

To: flambeau@darkcorp.com
From: hotspur@darkcorp.com
Subject: Your Assignment (Revised)

I'm pleased—pleased indeed—to inform you of two changes recently approved by the Low Command. First, your former mentor, Scraptus, has been banished to Siberia—literally. He now must learn to work in a parka with his new Russian clients. He's always bragged about his ability to innovate. Let's see what he can do with subjects too cold and hungry to do much more than drink themselves into a stupor every night.

Second, and more to the point, you're mine now, Flambeau. From here on, you'll do things my way or become the living embodiment of your own name: flame-basted Flambeau. Almost sounds like a menu item, doesn't it?

That doesn't mean you need to change any of the tactics Scraptus taught you. On the whole they are quite effective, but his constant insistence on taking the credit for the theories and practices developed by others exceeds even Our Exalted Baseness Below's tolerance for inflated egos.

Scraptus is clever, but he made one small mistake. He trusted someone. Some of his memos were leaked to a colleague, and they were passed along to Low Command. They came with the suggestion that you might be best suited to succeed him. You wouldn't have any idea how those memos got leaked, would you?

A fiend of my acquaintance down the chain of demand intercepted them and conferred with Slerchus (who is now in semi-retirement and only handling senior citizen scams). He assessed the situation and decided that Scraptus had become too arrogant for his own good. It was Slerchus who suggested that Scraptus was just the demon needed for our burgeoning Former Soviet Union Division.

Right now you're probably whining because you were next in line for his position. You were far too close to him for that to happen, Flambeau. Plus, like him, you're weak. That's why I own you now.

One thing I've noticed from reading the memos Scraptus sent you—you've been inefficient in your efforts to control your client Gene and to influence his peers at Glencrest. You need to tighten things up, redouble your efforts. Continue to use each of the "gifts." I want to see significant, far-reaching—yes, life-changing—results in your clients. Unless you succeed in a takeover soon, I can promise you'll understand all too well the reality of my name.

I expect a detailed takeover plan, complete with target dates, by next week.

>>NOTES<<

PREFACE

1. C. S. Lewis, *The Screwtape Letters* (New York: MacMillan, 1959), x.
2. Ibid., xiii.

CONFIDENTIAL MEMO TWO

1. Details in Exodus 15, PBP. I'll use the CBP designation whenever I refer you to their Current Business Plan and PBP for their Previous Business Plan.
2. See Numbers 12, PBP.
3. Numbers 12:2, PBP.

CONFIDENTIAL MEMO THREE

1. See 1 Samuel 18:17, PBP.
2. For details, see Genesis 3, PBP.

CONFIDENTIAL MEMO FOUR

1. See 1 Peter 4:15, CBP.
2. See Proverbs 11:13, PBP.
3. See 1 Timothy 5, CBP, for details.
4. See Proverbs 11:13, PBP.
5. See Leviticus 19:16, PBP.
6. See Proverbs 26:20, PBP.
7. See Proverbs 18:8 and 26:22, PBP.

CONFIDENTIAL MEMO FIVE

1. See James 3:1–10, CBP.
2. See James 1:26, CBP.
3. See Isaiah 50:4, PBP.

4. See Proverbs 15:2, PBP.
5. See Psalm 39:1–3, PBP.
6. See Proverbs 6:16–19, PBP—a delightful list of our "Top Seven" vices. Study it carefully.
7. See Proverbs 6:24, PBP.
8. See Jeremiah 18:18, PBP.
9. See Psalm 37:30, PBP.
10. See Proverbs 12:18, PBP
11. See Psalm 119:72, PBP.
12. See Proverbs 18:21, PBP.

CONFIDENTIAL MEMO SIX

1. See Isaiah 14, PBP.
2. See 3 John, CBP, for full details.
3. See 3 John 10, CBP.
4. See Luke 10:38–42, CBP.
5. See John 11:38–44, CBP.

CONFIDENTIAL MEMO SEVEN

1. See John 14:5, CBP.
2. See the Book of Haggai, PBP.
3. See Proverbs 17:22, PBP.
4. This is detailed in Numbers 14, PBP.

CONFIDENTIAL MEMO EIGHT

1. See 2 Timothy 1:15; 3:8; 4:14, CBP.
2. See 2 Timothy 1:6–8, CBP.
3. See 1 Timothy 6:3–4, CBP.
4. See Job 30:21, PBP.
5. For details, see Daniel 8–9, PBP.
6. See Daniel 8:12, PBP.
7. See Zechariah 3:1, PBP.

8. See 2 Timothy 2:25–26, CBP.
9. See Matthew 21:27–31, CBP.

CONFIDENTIAL MEMO NINE

1. See Luke 10:30–36, CBP.
2. See Acts 3–12, CBP.
3. See 1 Peter 5:8, CBP.
4. See Exodus 5–10, PBP.
5. See Numbers 16, PBP.
6. 1 Samuel 17, PBP.
7. See Judges 15, PBP.
8. These exploits are chronicled in 2 Samuel 13–16, PBP.
9. See Luke 9:54, CBP.
10. See John 18:10, CBP.
11. 1 Samuel 2, PBP.
12. 2 Samuel 15:11, PBP.

CONFIDENTIAL MEMO TEN

1. See John 11:16, CBP.
2. See John 14:5, CBP.

CONFIDENTIAL MEMO ELEVEN

1. 2 Timothy 1:6–8, CBP.
2. 2 Timothy 3:11–13, CBP.
3. Acts 26:28, CBP.

CONFIDENTIAL MEMO TWELVE

1. Genesis 38:13–25, PBP.
2. 2 Samuel 13:1–15, PBP.
3. Proverbs 2:16–19, PBP.
4. Proverbs 5:3–5, PBP.
5. Proverbs 5:6, PBP.

6. Proverbs 5:20–22, PBP.
7. These three are identified in Proverbs 6:24–25, PBP.
8. Proverbs 7:5–23, PBP.
9. 2 Timothy 3:6, CBP.
10. 1 Corinthians 7:1, CBP.
11. Matthew 5:27–28, CBP.
12. 1 Peter 3:1–4, CBP.

CONFIDENTIAL MEMO THIRTEEN

1. John 8:44, CBP.
2. Genesis 3:1–7, PBP.
3. Proverbs 6:17, CBP.
4. Proverbs 12:22, PBP.
5. Psalm 119:163, PBP.
6. Psalm 119:29, PBP.
7. Leviticus 6:1–6, PBP.
8. 1 Kings 13:18, PBP.
9. 2 Chronicles 18:3–5, 20–22, PBP.
10. Isaiah 59:3, 13, PBP.
11. Ephesians 4:25, CBP.
12. 2 Thessalonians 2:9–10, CBP.
13. Job 27:4, PBP.
14. Job 15:5, PBP.
15. Psalm 34:13, PBP.
16. Psalm 78:36, PBP.
17. Proverbs 6:17, PBP.
18. Jeremiah 9:5, PBP.
19. Jeremiah 9:8, PBP.
20. John 17:17, CBP.
21. Psalm 119:29, PBP.
22. Jeremiah 6:15; 8:12, PBP.